COWBOY'S DESTINY

SILVERSTONE DUDE RANCH - BOOK 9

APRIL MURDOCK

D1528248

APRIL MURDOCK BOOKS

Silverstone Dude Ranch

Cowboy's Redemption

Cowboy's Surprise

Cowboy's Competition

Cowboy's Fate

Cowboy's Challenge

Cowboy's Assumption

Cowboy's Myth

Cowboy's Rival

Cowboy's Destiny

Billionaire Ranchers Series

Impressing Her Billionaire Cowboy Boss

Keeping Her Billionaire Cowboy CEO

Saving Her Billionaire Cowboy Hero

Loving Her Billionaire Cowboy Partner

Arguing With Her Billionaire Cowboy

Teaching He Billionaire Cowboy Rookie

The Brothers of Thatcher Ranch

The Cowboy One and Only

The Cowboy City Girl

The Cowboy Troublemaker

The Cowboy' Second Chance

Wealth and Kinship

The Billionaire's Heart

The Billionaire's Hope

The Billionaire's Generosity

The Billionaire's Loyalty

The Billionaire's Sincerity

The Billionaire's Promise

Silverstone Ranch

The Movie Star Becomes a Cowboy

The Cowboy Gets a Second Chance

The Chef Chases His Cowboy Dream

The Billionaire Tries the Cowboy Life

The Royal Cowboy Chooses Love

Texas Redemption

A Long Road Home for the Broken Ranger

Sweet Second Chances for the Reluctant Billionaire

New Inspiration for the Lonely Rockstar

A Change of Plans for the Youngest Son

A Rude Awakening for the Ambitious Ex-Boyfriend

Small Town Billionaires

The Billionaire's High School Reunion

The Aimless Billionaire

The Billionaire's Charity Date

The Beach Bum Billionaire

The Grouchy Billionaire

The Billionaire's Home Town

Christmas Miracles

Her Undercover Billionaire Boss

The Billionaire's Family Christmas

Christmas Carols for the Billionaire

COWBOY'S DESTINY

SILVERSTONE DUDE RANCH - BOOK 9

APRIL MURDOCK

CHAPTER ONE

HOUSTON WHACKED THE MAGAZINE HE HELD IN HIS HAND with the back of his fingers. "Did you see this? It's *ridiculous*." He shook his head with disgust. "Just because a *few* people fell in love at some dude ranch doesn't make the place some kind of magical wonderland."

He lifted his gaze to meet his twin sister's.

Georgia couldn't look less interested. She had tilted her kitchen chair with her boots propped on the edge of the table, her gaze quickly scanning the words of her favorite romance novel.

His eyes narrowed. "Get your feet off the table. If Mom sees that—"

Her gray eyes flicked to meet his. "*Mom's* not here."

Houston elbowed her boots, pushing them from the table so they fell to the floor with a thump, followed by the legs of the chair.

She scowled at him but didn't return to her position. Instead, Georgia gave him an exaggerated sigh and tossed her book on the table. "What are you so upset about?"

He shook the magazine in his hand. "These columnists are writing *another* article about Silverstone Dude Ranch, and they're requesting that anyone who has fallen in love over there come back. They're offering an all-expenses paid weekend! Can you believe it? The things these places will come up with just to make a little extra money."

Houston dropped the magazine on the table with a slap.

"There's no reason Hickory Hollow couldn't become something like that," he insisted.

"We host events here. Why couldn't we claim this place makes people fall in love?"

Georgia snorted. "You remember the story of how Mom and Dad met, right?"

"What? Dad got hurt, Mom nursed him back to health. That's a perfectly fine love story."

His sister rolled her eyes and stood, placing her palms on the table while her eyes drilled into him. "She *hated* him. They were stuck here and had nothing better to do than fall in love. Is that the kind of reputation we want to have?" Her voice rose a few octaves and she straightened.

"Come to Hickory Hollow, where we combine the concept of an escape room with falling in love." She shook her head. "Sure. That sounds awesome." Sarcasm dripped from her tone as she reached across the table and grabbed her book. "Hickory Hollow isn't where people fall in love, Houston. If Silverstone Dude Ranch has figured out how to make it work, leave them alone. It's not like they're biting into our profit. This place makes plenty of money the way it is."

She spun on her heel and charged out of the kitchen.

With a huff, Houston settled back into his chair. He grabbed the article and was still studying it when the door to the back porch swung open. Kate headed straight for the cupboards, where she retrieved a glass for some lemonade.

She glanced over her shoulder at him and held up a second cup. "You want one?"

Practically an orphan, Kate had grown up running around Hickory Hollow with Houston and his sister, and she had always seemed comfortable in his home. His parents wouldn't have had it any other way.

She stared at him with expectation in her eyes, the glass in her hand.

"No thanks." He shook his head and held up the magazine. "Have you seen this article?"

Kate peered at him. "What article?"

"The one about that dude ranch about two hours away."

Her features brightened. "Oh! The one about the ranch that makes people fall in love? Yeah, isn't it sweet?" She wandered to the table and settled into a chair beside him, brown eyes dancing as she nodded to the magazine. "Apparently a lot of people are claiming it's totally legit."

He tossed the magazine aside. "It's a hoax is what it is. You don't fall in love because of the place. You fall in love because you're meant to be with that person." Houston gestured between them. "Take us, for example. You're like a sister to me. We went through our awkward stages together. And you're so not my type. It would take more than just visiting that ranch together to make us fall in love. See? Ridiculous."

The excitement in her gaze dimmed somewhat. She put her glass on the table and reached for the magazine. "I don't know. I think it's sweet." Her lips lifted into a smile. "Being caught off guard by someone you didn't realize was perfect for you…"

Her gaze lifted to his. She blushed and, after returning the magazine to its spot on the table, she ran a hand through her short, pixie-style hair with a shrug.

"Besides, it's not like there's anything you or anyone else can do about it." Kate snickered. "You can't just call the magazine and tell them you've found your soulmate at that ranch and then reveal that you pulled one over on them."

His eyes widened. "Why not?"

She stiffened. "Huh?"

Houston leaned toward her, causing her to edge away from him. "Why *couldn't* we submit a form and head out to that ranch? It's not like we'd *fall in love* with each other. Then, after the weekend, we could tell them just how wrong they are."

Frowning, she moved her hand through her hair again. "I don't know…"

He shifted closer to her. "Come on, Kate. It could be fun. We wouldn't have to pay anything, and we could get an idea of how they run things over there. What do you have to lose?"

Okay, so this plan could be executed better. And his mother wouldn't approve if she knew why he wanted to go to Silverstone Ranch, so he'd have to come up with another, more legitimate reason.

Kate fidgeted in her seat and retrieved her glass. As she brought it to her lips, her gaze darted away from him. "I just don't see how doing something like that would benefit—"

Letting out an exaggerated breath, Houston leaned back in his chair once more. "It's the principle of the thing. People are going to read that article and believe visiting that place is all they need to do to have a happy relationship. How many marriages will end in divorce just because people fall for this hype? If we go out there and prove they're wrong, we'd be helping hundreds of future relationships."

Kate nibbled on her lower lip. Her focus bounced around the room before landing on him again. "But what about what we have to do out here? You have horses to look after and I have—"

"I'll figure out something." He jumped up from his chair and snatched the magazine from the table. Rolling it into a tube, he tapped it on her shoulder. "Thanks for coming with me, Kate. This is going to be great!"

He made his way through the kitchen and out into the hallway.

It shouldn't be too hard to come up with a good excuse. In fact, he could probably even convince his mother that it was a business trip and then could get paid to go. No, that was less likely.

Still, there was good point to all of this. If he went out to Silverstone, not only could he get the writers to retract their article, but he might be able to get them to do a spread on their little piece of Texas.

CHAPTER TWO

KATE BLEW OUT A BREATH THROUGH PURSED LIPS. SHE HADN'T exactly agreed to participating in this whole charade with Houston, and yet somehow, she'd been roped into it like he'd lassoed her. But she wasn't some steer that he could drag around.

She rolled the glass of lemonade between both her palms, staring at the yellow liquid as it rippled with the motion. Saying no to Houston wasn't easy. Both he and Georgia had a way of making her agree to things when normally, she would have just walked away.

A sigh escaped her and she took a sip of her drink. There were worse things than going on a vacation with Houston. He was fun to spend time with. And he was right, they were just like siblings. It'd be nice to get off Hickory Hollow property and see what else was out there—even if it was just another ranch that did the same stuff.

The empty room felt larger, somehow, now that Houston had left. The second he'd mentioned that they'd never fall for each other, the air had shifted. What if the article was right? What if there was some kind of magical power that seemed to grow at Silverstone Ranch, and it was causing unlikely matches to fall head over heels in love? Swallowing hard, she glanced at the door Houston had exited through. He could be wrong. They could go and she'd find she had latent feelings for him.

Kate huffed. That was about as likely as her growing a pair of horns on her head. Getting to her feet, she crossed the room and placed her empty glass in the sink. There was no guarantee that Houston would be accepted for the event, anyway. People didn't just offer free vacations without vetting the people who submitted a request. She was just overthinking this. If he managed to get picked for a trip to that ranch, they'd go and have some fun and that would be that. Nothing more.

They'd come right back and nothing would change. Kate turned around and leaned against the farmhouse sink, her hands resting on the porcelain as her eyes swept the room. When she was a kid, this place had felt like a real-life castle. There was so much space, and the ceilings were so tall. Houston and Georgia, though they hadn't wanted for anything, were still taught to work hard and they managed to be down to earth despite the money they would likely inherit.

And then, there was Kate. She didn't remember her parents, who had passed away in an accident when she was about six. It was easier to catch glimpses of them in her dreams. But the moment she woke up, those memories disappeared.

All she knew was that after the accident, she'd been brought to Hickory Hollow to live with her great uncle. He worked the ranch and the owners had allowed Kate to stay with him and help out. By the time Uncle Ted had passed away, she was sixteen and she'd chosen to stay. Hickory Hollow was more of a home than anywhere else. And she loved working for Dakota and Brady.

Growing up on the ranch meant she spent a lot of time with the owners' kids. She'd always been envious of Georgia—Houston, too. It wasn't just the house and the legacy that accompanied it. It was their family, their cousins, everyone in their lives who supported and pushed them to achieve their greatest potential.

And what did she have? Nothing. No one.

That wasn't really fair. The Shipley family had accepted her as much as one would accept an orphan. Dakota and Brady had been wonderful surrogate parents even before her uncle had passed away. They just weren't *her* parents.

She pushed away from the sink and headed for the door. Had Georgia been around, Kate would have asked her opinion. Knowing Georgia, she would have disagreed with Houston. They might be twins but they were as different as could be. She'd argue with her brother for the heck of it.

Yep, it would be best to leave Georgia out of this. Whatever happened, Kate would keep it to herself.

"KATE. KATE, WE'RE HERE."

A deep voice dragged her from her sleep. Kate yawned, blinked, and looked around, her focus hazy. She hadn't intended to drift off for that little catnap. Through the truck windows, her gaze landed immediately on a large brick house.

"I thought we were supposed to be staying in some kind of cottage. That place looks bigger than the house at Hickory Hollow."

Houston ducked, staring through the front window at the house. "I don't think we'll be staying there. That's just where we check in."

She lifted a brow. "We're checking in at someone's house? Isn't that a little weird?"

He pulled out a sheet of paper and scanned it. "We're here to meet with Ben Greene and Jake and Amelia Spencer." Houston looked up at Kate. "I think one of them lives here and the other two are the columnists."

"How did our application get approved, anyway? Didn't they check if you've actually been here before?"

Houston flashed her a smile. "I have a connection with one of the ranch hands, who was able to fake some stuff for me before our application got to the columnists." He tucked the paper into a backpack that sat between them. "You ready?"

Her focus hadn't left the house. What would it have been like to grow up in a place like this? It almost looked like a mansion. The more of the world she saw, the more she realized just how small she was and what she would miss out on if she didn't venture beyond Hickory Hollow.

"Kate? You ready?"

She jumped and turned to face Houston. "Right. Yeah, okay."

He grinned. "Remember. We're newly married and we met and fell in love here."

Her brows creased. "Wouldn't it be easier to play this as close to real as possible? What if we tell them that we knew each other growing up and we finally realized we were in love when we were here? Then we wouldn't have to avoid talking about how we met. The only difference is that we're not actually together."

He shrugged. "I guess that would be fine, too. Just so long as we don't deviate from the fact that Silverstone is the place that made us fall in love. At the end of this little visit, we're going to announce to the writers, the people who work here, and everyone who came to this dumb event that they were all duped."

Her stomach knotted. Somehow, the way he phrased it made it sound like they weren't helping anyone out at all. He was rubbing this in their faces. She swallowed hard and climbed out of the car as he did. It was fine. Houston was just excited. That was all. He wanted to make a difference; he'd said so himself. She was probably just nervous.

Kate shut her door and opened the back door to the cab, pulling out her tattered duffle bag and slinging it over her shoulder. Houston opened the door on the other side and flashed her a smile.

She offered a half-hearted one in return before shutting the door and turning toward the large home. It really was breathtaking. It was too bad the journalists had this all wrong. Otherwise, she would have loved to come to this place to find her true love.

Houston came up beside her, placing his hand on the small of her back as they headed toward the house. A handful of other cars and trucks were already parked out front. Were they the last ones to arrive? She prayed they weren't. Already she was getting anxiety about being put on the spot.

Kate was a wallflower in every sense of the word. Even in high school, she'd followed Georgia and Houston around like she was their literal shadow.

Her booted foot landed on the wooden step and a spark of fear shot up her spine. She couldn't do this. Kate spun around, away from Houston, and retreated a few steps back. He turned and faced her with confusion emanating from his gray eyes.

His brows eased as he frowned. "Is there something wrong?"

She shook her head, then nodded. "Yes. I can't do it. You should have picked someone else. I can't go in there and pretend to be something I'm not."

Houston headed down the stairs, his features softening. "But you're not pretending to be something you're not. I'm not asking you to pretend anything. Well, except that you love me. But you've already do right?"

Kate lifted her gaze to meet Houston's. "You do?"

He laughed and placed both his hands on her shoulders. "Of course I do. We've spent our whole lives together. You can't do that and not develop some kind of feelings for the other person. I might get annoyed with you—and Georgia, for that matter—but I still love you. I would lay down my life to protect you. Heck, when that right guy comes along to sweep you off your feet, I'll be the one holding a shotgun telling him he'd better not break your heart." His broad smile eased her racing heart somewhat. He brushed his knuckles against her chin. "Now, let's go in there and see what we can do to debunk this whole thing."

Houston grabbed her hand and led her, once again, up the steps toward the front door. This was it. There would be no going back after this. Once they stepped over that threshold, she'd be participating in a scam of sorts.

But it was to help others, right? That was the whole reason she'd agreed to this whole mess.

Kate sighed, clutching onto Houston's hand a little tighter. Yes, she'd follow through. How could she not? She loved Houston. Even when he was acting a little crazy.

CHAPTER THREE

HOUSTON KNOCKED ON THE DOOR TO THE LARGE RANCH house, his body humming with nervous energy. If he pulled this off, then maybe they could put Hickory Hollow on the map for more than just horse training and boarding. He'd always felt his parents could have done more with their family ranch. Even Aunt Annie was able to turn Bolton Farms into a place that drew new customers. Yes, they were all linked, but he couldn't help feeling like there should be more excitement. What if they could gather people for larger events? There was definitely room for it.

The door opened and an older gentleman with graying hair beamed at them. The lines around his eyes were deep, showing years of hard work but adding onto that a semblance of joy. His entire countenance made Houston feel welcome, as if there was no doubt he belonged there.

The man held out his hand and beamed at Houston. "Welcome. You must be here for the article." His focus shifted to Kate, then bounced back to Houston. "Well, don't just stand out there. Take my hand, my boy, and come meet the others."

Houston shook the man's hand and was almost immediately yanked into the foyer of the house. The door shut behind them almost like they were being locked into a jail cell. Kate's hand still clutched his, and he bit back a smile.

He leaned closer to her and murmured, "Don't worry, it will all work out. You're doing great."

They followed the older man, who hadn't given them his name. But if Houston had to guess, he would say this was the Ben Greene listed on the informational paper. They moved through the house until they came to a large kitchen where several people lingered, chatting with each other. There had to be close to thirty people in the room. Some held drinks while others had plates in their hands, piled high with some of the refreshments spread out on the table.

The low hum of conversation sounded more like a hive of bees than a group of people chatting. Kate remained close, her body pressed up against him like a scared pup.

The man who'd let them in turned around and smiled again. "You can put your luggage there." He pointed to a corner of the room where only a handful of suitcases sat. "We'll have your belongings sent out to the place you'll be staying once we figure out where you'll be. Some people have already been assigned. Until then, you can visit with the others and get something to eat. We'll be getting started shortly."

Kate stood on her toes and murmured, "Are you sure about this? We could probably duck out and leave. There are so many people here, I bet they wouldn't even notice."

Houston shook his head. "Come on, Kate. This is going to be fun. And we'll be helping people. We just can't do that until we figure out how they're doing it. Try to relax a little. We can go mingle with everyone like he said."

He dropped his duffle on the floor and motioned for her to do the same before they moved farther into the kitchen. A few guests turned their way, offering smiles, but no one approached. That was just as well. He'd rather observe these people a little before deciding how to proceed.

Kate didn't leave his side, so he led them to the table where they could get plates. The spread reminded him of what might be served at a reception for a wedding—cold-cut sliders, vegetables with dip, fruit, and crackers with cheese. There was even a section piled high with sweets.

He dipped his head and whispered, "I hear they have a five-star chef who prepares meals here."

Her eyes widened and scanned the table of food. "That's amazing."

"More like overkill. Who needs a five-star chef at a ranch? I don't care if it is a dude ranch. People who work around horses don't need fancy meals."

A male chuckle startled both of them. Houston glanced up to find an amused gentleman who wore a cowboy hat standing across from them at the table.

He picked up a cherry tomato and popped it into his mouth. "They didn't hire the five-star chef."

Houston gave the man a disbelieving look. "So, the guy works for free? That doesn't sound right. What are they doing? Holding him against his will?"

The guy chuckled again and shook his head. "He fell in love with the owner's daughter."

"That's even worse."

A sharp elbow dug into Houston's side as the man's eyes narrowed.

Houston bit back a yelp and his gaze shot to Kate, who shook her head. Right. He wasn't supposed to share his disbelief about finding love here. He was supposed to be one of the people who had found the love of his life right here on this ranch. He forced a smile and laughed.

"I mean, that's lucky. One more thing to put this place on the map, right?"

The man tilted his head and grabbed another cherry tomato. "I think it's the movie star and the billionaire who married the other daughters that made more of a difference. Then again, it could be the prince."

Houston choked on the cracker in his mouth. Kate patted his back.

"That's so romantic," she said. "How did the prince end up finding love at a place like this?"

The man shrugged. "I'm gonna guess it's the same as any one of you guys. For me, I knew the girl I married since we were kids. We were best friends, and when I came back to town, I knew there was nothing else that would hold me back from being with her. So, I stayed."

Kate crooned. "That's exactly why this place is perfect for finding love. Because of stories like that." She glanced around the room. "Which one is your wife?"

He pointed to a woman who was standing beside the older man who'd let them in. "She's talking to her father over there."

Both Houston and Kate looked in the direction he pointed, and Houston's eyes grew wide. "Wait a minute. So you're telling me you're one of the guys who married his daughters?"

Amused, the man nodded.

"Which one are you? The movie star, the prince, or the billionaire?"

"I'm the chef." He tossed back another tomato and winked at Kate. "I hope you guys enjoy your stay. If you have any special requests for meals, let me know and I'll see what I can do to make that happen. You folks are all our honored guests this week."

Houston gaped after him as the chef wandered over to his wife and pressed a kiss to her cheek. She smiled at him with the most loving expression Houston had ever seen.

Kate elbowed him again.

"Hey, why do you keep doing that?"

"See?" She nodded to the couple. "People *do* fall in love here."

He shook his head. "You heard his story. He knew his wife long before he came here. They grew up together. That doesn't count. This place is claiming that even strangers might fall in love while they're here."

"But you and I have known each other since we were kids and you don't think we'll fall in love—that way." Her cheeks filled with color. "I mean, there has to be something about this place, right? The authors of that column noticed *something*. That's why they're offering to have all these people come out for this updated article."

"I don't buy it. Maybe the people here are plants. We'll get to the bottom of it. People don't just fall in love with strangers or even people they know unless they're primed for it." He moved away from her a step. "I'm going to visit with some people. You want to come?"

She shook her head, pointing to the table. "I think I'll get something to eat and wait until they start their thing."

He nodded, offering her a reassuring smile. "Sure. I'll be back."

His gaze swept over the room. So, they were including the owner's daughters in this article. That didn't seem fair. It seemed strange that every one of the girls married someone famous. If Hickory Hollow had a movie star, a prince, a five star chef, and a billionaire constantly on site, then sure, they would have more people coming out to see the place.

Just because people were falling in love right and left didn't mean the ranch was responsible. People fell in love at famous theme parks all the time. It didn't mean *those* places were hot spots for love. The only place he could think of that qualified as a "love" destination was Vegas. That place claimed thousands of hearts every year. And to be fair, a lot of those relationships ended before the year was out.

He wandered past a few people talking and paused to overhear their conversation.

"We fell in love a few months ago. It was a work retreat."

A male voice chuckled. "Yeah. She couldn't stand me. But look at us now." He gave her a warm smile. "We were meant to be together and we just didn't see it. I joke that the barn out there had something to do with it. When we got stuck in that thing, there was no holding us back."

Houston snorted, moving through the room while he continued to listen.

"How did you two meet?"

A tall man with brown hair dressed in some kind of uniform leaned forward. "Oh, you don't want to know."

Laughs from the group.

A pretty girl waved her hand in the air and glanced at the man beside her. "Couldn't be as bad as our situation. He thought I was someone else he'd hired to be his fake girlfriend."

The first man commented once more. "I was going to con her into falling in love with me."

The group went quiet. Then, the woman standing next to the one who had just spoken let out a laugh. "It's not as bad as all that. I ended up hiring him to be my fake husband to get out of an arranged marriage. Turns out we fell for each other before any of that came out. It's a crazy story, but it turned out for the best."

These people were *all* crazy. Paying people to be in fake relationships. Con artists. Childhood friends who didn't know they were in love. None of it made any sense. They *had* to be plants.

A woman stood at the front of the group and clinked the glass in her hand. She smiled broadly and waited for the group of people to settle down before speaking.

"Hello, everyone, and thank you so much for coming! This weekend, we're going to be having a lot of fun, but we will also be interviewing each of you so you can tell us your story. This article has been approved for an entire issue for our upcoming magazine release. We're going to dive into why you two weren't together to begin with, if you knew each other before, and if you didn't, what made you fall in love. We'll be discussing how the ranch played a part, whether it was because you spoke with one of the owners or if you didn't have any interaction with them and it was the property itself."

She let out a soft laugh, then held out her hand to someone who came to stand beside her. "We believe there is something special here and we want to share that with the world. So, this week, you're going to stay in special cabins that have been set up for you. Some are larger than others, so you might be sharing with another couple. But there is plenty of space and you will be able to have your own rooms. If you need special accommodations, you can speak to Ben Greene over there." She gestured toward the older man who had let them in. Houston had guessed right.

"Tonight, we will be sharing a meal in the cafeteria, but don't worry. It's going to be special. We have a five-star chef on site, and he's got a spectacular menu planned. Until then, please enjoy yourselves."

The group of people cheered. All the faces were happy and excited. Houston glanced back at Kate, who looked like she had seen a ghost.

CHAPTER FOUR

Kate was frozen. She couldn't move. Everything that woman had just said sounded awful. Kate didn't like people. Not strangers, anyway. She didn't want to mingle and talk with anyone. She would prefer to stay holed up in her hotel room or wherever they were going to be put and avoid contact with everyone. Houston could do all the work.

All he'd said he needed her for was to pretend that he had a fiancée or a wife. Wait, which were they? They were supposed to be together, but she couldn't remember what he'd said she was supposed to be to him.

Her anxiety deepened. If Houston had said they were married, didn't that mean they would be assigned a room to share? How was she supposed to share a room with Houston? Her breathing became sharp and stilted. She couldn't share a room with Houston. Especially not in front of other people. If they were going to be put in the same space as another couple, they'd have to show more affection to each other.

She liked he pace and her rivacy. She needed it.

Out of now re, Houston aterialized in front of her. He took her ha l and led her out of the room and into the dim hallway

"Hey," he m mured. "Wh 's the matter?"

Her wide e s landed on n as she continued breathing fast. "I shou n't have com with you. We shouldn't have done this. I n't—"

He pulled h into a hug a inst his chest and she sucked in a breath. e rubbed her ck.

"You are the erfect perso r this little undercover thing we're doing ou're going t e just fine. I know it."

She shook r head, rubb g her nose against his chest. Her muffle words were obably unintelligible to him. "What if I n ke a mistake nd blow this whole thing for you? What they make u stay in the same room? You don't want t have to—"

He chuckle the sound vi ating from his chest. "You're worrying to much. They bably will put us in the same room becaus I told them were married."

She pulled ck and stare at him. "Why would you *do* that? You s uld have kn n they would put us in the same room d I need—I c 't—"

He placed h finger on he ps. "It's fine. I'll sleep on the couch or a air. Heck, I'll eep on the floor if I have to. This is my ng, and I ge hat you didn't really sign up for any of is. I'll make ire you're comfortable." His dark eyes pe ed at her, stu ing her. "Do you trust me?"

"Of course I do. I just—"

"Then it will be fine." He hugged her again, tight.

The tension and anxiety seemed to float away from her, rising into the air before being swept away. It was the strangest sensation she had ever experienced.

When Houston pulled back from her, the warmth and security she'd enjoyed while being held by him left. The cool air surrounded her instead, making her feel chilled. She rubbed her arms as she watched him head back into the kitchen. Slowly, she followed.

Okay. She'd be okay. She did trust him; she always had. Besides, this event was only going to be a few days. She could handle a few days in a strange place with strange people. It wasn't like any of them would know what was really going on. Not until Houston made his big reveal.

Kate stood in the doorway of the kitchen and watched the groups of people. They made it all look so easy. How were they able to just visit with people and not have a care in the world? She always felt like she was outside looking in wherever she went. The only people she ever felt comfortable with were the Shipleys.

It wasn't that she hadn't tried changing. She really had. She'd forced herself to get out of her box several times. But each time, she ended up having a panic attack just like Houston had witnessed.

Her stomach lurched as she realized he probably wasn't the only one who had noticed. Any one of these people could have taken note, and now they might be talking about her. T[ ] nausea roil[ ] in her stomach once more as she shrunk [ ]ck against the[ ] [ ]all.

Houston wa[ ] on the far si[ ] of the room already, chatting with the wo[ ]an who had [ ]en them all their information. She smiled [ ] she spoke v[ ]h him, and he did the same. He'd alway[ ] [ ]een popular, [ ]ever having had a hard time making frie[ ][ ]s. She'd lost [ ]ack of all the girls who had either dated [ ]im or throw[ ] [ ]hemselves at him when they were in high[ ] [ ]chool. Even i[ ] [ ]ollege, he'd come home with a new girl e[ ]h time.

None of the[ ] lasted very l[ ] g. But they were all the same. Tall, beautif[ ] ... blonde.

Kate lifted h[ ] hand to her [ ]n mousy brown hair and she sighed. She [ ] long ago a[ ] pted that she was different from most [ ] the other gi[ ] she knew. She never dated anyone. It [ ]s just the w[ ] things were. One day, she thought she [ ]ight find son[ ]ne who would accept her for who she w[ ] but it wasn[ ] likely. Not with the way she seemed to d[ ]appear again[ ] the wall whenever she was in a room with [ ]ts of people.

No, she'd ju[ ] live her life [ ] the ranch and do the work no one else wa[ ] d to do.

A woman [ ]anced in he[ ] direction and smiled. Kate offered a ti[ ]id smile in [ ]turn but continued to lean against the [ ]ll where she [ ]ood. In a few more minutes, they'd prob[ ]ly be taken t[ ] the places where they would be staying. [ ]til then, she'[ ] ust watch.

The woman [ ]ho smiled w[ ]dered away from her group and headed [ ]raight towar[ ] [ ]er.

Kate stiffened. Her gaze darted from side to side. The only escape was through the door to her right and if she took it, she'd be heading into the main living space of Ben Greene's home. That concept caused her even more anxiety. He hadn't invited her to come into his *house*. He'd only allowed her entrance to this part. She couldn't just go wandering.

On the other side of the room, there was a door that appeared to lead to the open air she was craving. But she would never get there before the woman met her. Kate fidgeted with her hands and shifted her weight from one foot to the other. She probably looked like she was dancing. Wait, she could go to the right and try to make a beeline for the front door of the house. Then, she could wait outside.

Kate took a step toward the exit only to be cut off.

"Hey, what's your name?"

She froze, her feet glued to the spot. Slowly, her head swiveled around and she came face to face with a woman who had blonde hair and blue eyes. She looked like she could be a model.

She smiled widely at Kate and held out her hand. "I'm Avery."

Tentatively, Kate accepted the woman's hand. It was silky soft, not the hand of someone who was familiar with heavy labor. Kate withdrew as fast as her hand would allow. She rubbed her callused hand on her jeans and smiled, though the action probably looked more like a grimace.

"Kate."

"Hello, Kate. So, you gonna tell me why you look like a frightened little rabbit all the way over here by yourself?"

Kate flushed. She searched the room for Houston, praying he'd come to rescue her from this situation. But he had moved to speak to someone else, and he was laughing. Great. He was having the time of his life and that meant he wouldn't even register that she was present.

Letting out a sigh, Kate dared her eyes to meet Avery's before dropping her gaze to the ground. "I'm not very good with people. Or large groups."

Understanding filled Avery's blue eyes. "Ah, that makes sense." She took a step back, probably giving Kate some space on purpose. "What do you do for work?"

"I work on a ranch."

Avery brightened. "Here? I heard there were some of us who did."

Kate shook her head quickly. "No, I actually work at a ranch a few hours away."

She didn't look the least bit disappointed. "Really? That's neat. I bet there are a lot of ranches in this area. There's so much open space."

Kate's grin came more easily this time. "I suppose so."

"I'm a realtor," Avery offered without being asked. "We came out here a few months ago for a corporate retreat. It was so much fun." She gave Kate a side-eyed look. "But then I guess this isn't the kind of place you'd come for fun, right? It's just like more work."

Kate let out a soft laugh. "For me, it's fun because I *don't* have to work. I can just enjoy the atmosphere."

Avery beamed. "That's interesting. What do you like most about it?"

Kate stiffened. She hadn't been here before. She didn't even know anything besides the fact that people came here to find love. This place was supposedly really big and had a lot to offer. What was she supposed to say?

"I loved the hotel, but technically it isn't part of the dude ranch experience." Avery folded her arms and glanced at Kate again. "But when we were here, my favorite part was the archery. I got pretty good at it." She let out a laugh and fiddled with her hair. "I bet you'd be pretty good with lassoing, right?"

Kate's brows creased.

"Because you're a rancher. I tried my hand at that, but I wasn't that great." Her eyes widened and she reached out to touch Kate's arm. "I'm so sorry. I'm talking too much, aren't I? I should have known better. I bet you'd like some peace and quiet, right? Well, there should be a lot of that, too. I hear we're going to go on an evening ride after dinner. That will give you plenty of space."

She offered Kate one more smile. "This will be fun. Don't worry too much about it. And if you ever find you need a friend or someone to talk to, you can come find me."

Kate nodded as Avery headed back toward her group. She looked back and winked at Kate but didn't seem to be talking about her at all. No one else in her small group was looking in Kate's direction.

Breathing a sigh of relief, Kate let her eyes close briefly before opening them to find Houston standing in front of her. She gasped and instinctively slugged him in the arm.

"Why did you do that?"

Houston laughed, rubbing his arm. "I didn't do anything. *You* closed your eyes." He glanced over his shoulder toward the people. "Who were you talking to?"

Kate's gaze trailed back over to Avery. "Her name is Avery."

"Did you find out anything interesting about her?"

She shrugged. "She came here for a corporate retreat, so she probably fell in love with a co-worker. I don't know, though. She was more interested in talking about the activities they offer here."

Houston grunted. "I talked with the writer and then I talked with some guy who works here. He ended up getting together with someone he knew from before working here, too. Seems split pretty evenly between people who already knew each other and complete strangers that met and fell in love." He pointed out a group near Avery's. "There's a con artist in that group. Literally, a guy who was going to con the woman he married into falling for him. But it ended up 'not as bad as it sounds.'"

The shocked and borderline disgruntled look Kate knew must have been on her face triggered his laugh. Houston shook his head. "I know, right? The more I learn about these people, the more I can't believe it. You know the shows on HGTV are fake. Reality TV shows, too. Why couldn't this be the same? I just can't figure out who is pulling all the strings. I don't doubt that these people are actually in love or married, but I do think they're playing a part."

Kate looked over at Avery again. She had been very nice. It didn't seem like she was capable of something so deceptive. But then again, Kate wasn't a particularly good judge of character most of the time. She would probably be better off just sticking with Houston.

"Alright, you two. We have your cabin all situated. Grab your duffels and we'll retrieve the other couple." A woman with short brown hair held a clipboard in her arms as she looked from Kate to Houston. "You're the Shipleys, right?"

Houston frowned. "We're sharing a cabin with someone else?"

The woman nodded. "Unfortunately, we don't have enough for everyone to have their own. There are other guests here this weekend and they'd already booked their cabins. But don't worry, each of you will have your own rooms. You'll just share the common areas." She looked again from Kate to Houston. "I have you sharing a cabin with Harper and Lucas Bailey. Will that be okay?"

Before Kate could ask for them to be placed with Avery or on their own, Houston flashed his charming smile. "That will be perfect."

A smile crossed the woman's face. "Okay. Let's get going."

Houston grabbed both duffle bags and started after the woman. He stopped after a few steps and looked back at Kate, jerking his head toward the back door. "You coming?"

It wasn't like she had any other choice.

CHAPTER FIVE

HOUSTON FOLLOWED THE WOMAN AND THE OTHER COUPLE past a barn, several corrals, and up a trail leading to a cluster of small cottages. Some looked big enough for larger parties while others were so small, they probably resembled hotel suites.

He exchanged an excited look with Kate as they drew closer, but she seemed less than enthused. Hopefully she would warm up. He'd never witnessed this kind of reaction from her before. She'd always been content at the ranch. He'd just have to figure out a way to get her out of her shell.

Moving closer to her, he adjusted the straps on his shoulder and grinned. "These guys seem nice. It will be cool to get to know them a little better. What do you think?"

Kate shrugged. "I liked Avery."

"I'm sure she'll be around, too. Hey, they said we could choose to do something on our own for the next few hours. Dinner will be at five, so that gives us about two hours to poke around and see what they have going on. Did you notice that hotel on our way out this way? I hear they have a pool and some great gardens. I bet we could use that stuff since we're guests here."

She shrugged again. "I think I might just stay inside and read a book or something."

He frowned, putting more distance between themselves and their companions "Kate, the whole point of coming is to get to know people here and participate with everyone. We can't do that if all you want to do is hang out in the cottage."

Her scowl matched his and she lowered her voice. "I didn't want to come to this thing to do whatever you're planning, anyway. I did because we're friends. This whole plan of yours is going to blow up in your face, and then what are you going to do? I'd rather let you do that on your own."

His mouth dropped open. "What?"

She grimaced. "Sorry. I'm just really uncomfortable right now. I don't know anyone, and I don't care to. I just want to keep to myself."

Houston nodded. "Okay. Well, how about instead of doing something with someone else, you and I can go get horses and explore the trails. You like riding."

If he was going to get her to be more at ease while they were here, then he'd have to make sure to offer her activities that did that. She liked riding and nature. She was good with the animals. Kate was even good with the people at the ranch back home. This side of her was something new. He'd have to call Georgia and see if she knew anything about it.

He continued watching Kate, hoping she'd give him an indication that his idea was acceptable before they got to the cottage and had to deal with the other couple. She didn't want to be put on the spot for any reason. The other couple was married, so they'd get a room to themselves. If Kate and Houston were lucky, the place would have three rooms and they could split up. There were always reasonable explanations for things like that. However, if there were only two rooms, they would have to quietly figure out a sleeping arrangement.

Kate's shoulders relaxed. It was a small movement, but he could see it. She was bending, accepting his terms. A short nod was all he got before they arrived at the door.

The woman with the clipboard held out a key to the other couple and then to Houston. "Enjoy your stay!" She swung open the door but remained outside. "I'll let you guys figure out which room you want to claim. Dinner will be at five sharp, followed by an evening trail ride."

She headed back down the trail toward the main one. The other couple headed inside first. Houston gestured for Kate to head in next, but she shook her head.

"It's fine. I'll go first." He followed the others in and heard Kate shuffling behind him.

The cottage was decorated simply. There was a couch and chairs in the living room surrounding a coffee table. A fireplace on the far side of the room didn't look like it had ever been used—either it was too warm here, or they were really good about cleaning it. A small table near the kitchen was surrounded by four chairs, and the kitchen had a little and and a few cupboards, with a full-sized refrigerator. A hallway that led toward a few doors was the only way to go.

Lucas and Harper hovered in the living room, looking around. Lucas glanced up and met Houston's gaze. "How about we take a look at the sleeping situations?"

Houston grinned. "Sounds great." He looked over his shoulder at Kate, who hadn't moved from her place at the door. "You want to come, sweetie?"

She shook her head. "Later. I think I'll get a drink of water."

Houston nodded. "Okay. Be right back."

He moved down the hall after Lucas. Harper ended up staying back as well, mentioning something about a drink of water sounding good. There were two bedrooms. Lucas went into the first room as Houston ducked his head inside. This room didn't have an adjoining bathroom. It must not be the master suite.

Lucas met Houston's gaze as he dropped his bag on the bed. "You can have the other one."

Houston snickered. "I don't have to have the bigger room. We could flip a coin for it."

Lucas moved toward the window. "Nah, this place is great. Besides, I feel like you two could use the extra peace and quiet."

Kate would hate it if she knew Lucas had noticed her unease. Then again, she likely already knew people had clued in to it. Everyone here had been more outgoing. She did seem like the odd duck.

"She gets anxious around people she doesn't know well." At least, that was what he thought. It was the only thing that made sense at this point.

Lucas held up his hands. "No judgment. It's okay. A lot more people than you realize deal with that sort of thing. If she warms up to us, great. If not, we won't push her."

Houston nodded with appreciation. "Thanks." He watched Lucas dig through his bag on the edge of the queen bed. "So, how did you and Harper meet?"

Lucas shot Houston a look from his position and smiled. "We were high school sweethearts. We actually fell in love and got engaged before we wound up here."

Houston's brows pinched and he moved farther into the room. "That doesn't make sense. I thought everyone here was supposed to be single before they came and ended up getting married after the fact."

He let out a laugh. "We were no different. We *were* engaged, but she left me at the altar."

Houston sucked in a breath and glanced back at the door. "Ouch. What happened?"

Lucas dropped what he was doing and faced Houston. He shoved his hands into his pockets and glanced at the ceiling before he brought this gaze back to meet Houston's eyes. "She was pregnant when she left, but she didn't tell me. Then, she came back here to visit one of her friends, and I happened to be here at the same time. We ended up reconciling.'

Houston didn't think his eyes could have gotten any bigger. He probably resembled a bug more than a person at this point. Wow. That's pretty—"

"Miraculous." Lucas nodded toward Houston. "What about you two?"

"Us? Oh, we've known each other since we were kids. Best friends and all that, you know?"

Lucas nodded. "Similar state to mine, I would wager."

"Yeah. Pretty close." Houston rubbed the back of his neck and jerked his chin toward the door. "I guess I should go check out that other room before the girls come asking why we aren't settled yet."

He backed away and headed down the hall past a small bathroom and into a larger room. A king-size four-poster bed was against one wall, two small tables with lamps positioned on either side. A chaise longue sat near the bed, and an armoire stood a few feet away from that. A doorway opened up to a tiled space. Houston dropped both bags at the foot of the bed and went into the bathroom. The space was bigger than he'd expected with a jetted tub, a walk-in shower, and a small linen closet.

The cottage had appeared smaller on the outside. This place was luxurious. If this was what they offered on the ranch side, then what must the hotel be like?

"Wow," Kate's voice whispered from behind him.

Houston whirled around and beamed at her. "Pretty great, right?"

Her large doe eyes were soaking up every last bit of tile and glittery surface. She nodded and wandered over to the granite countertops. "Do you think this is one of the nicer ones? We passed some pretty small cottages before we got here."

"Probably. I can't imagine they'd have something like this for their run-of-the-mill visitors."

Her eyes stopped trailing over the bathroom and landed on him. "There are only two rooms."

He knew exactly what she was referring to. There weren't two beds.

Houston moved closer to her, then past her into the bedroom. He shut the bedroom door and she came out of the bathroom just as they had their privacy.

"See that chaise? I'll sleep there. You can have the whole king bed to yourself. And there's a door on the bathroom, so we can change in there. See? This all worked out."

The skepticism was still plastered on her face, but she didn't argue.

"Get yourself settled and then we'll go for a walk or a ride. I know they have a ride scheduled for us after dinner, but if you want to do that twice, I don't mind. Those gardens I mentioned before sound like something that could help ease your anxiety."

Her gaze shot to meet his and her face flushed. She didn't like people noticing her struggles. It made sense—he didn't like people knowing his weaknesses, either.

He moved across the room again and placed his hands on her upper arms. "Don't worry. It's all working out exactly as I expected. I can't think of one way this will—how did you say it?— blow up in our faces."

The color in her cheeks deepened and she pulled away from him. "I'm going to do my best to believe you. Just promise me that you won't put me on the spot in front of anyone. I don't think I can promise to not freak out."

"Deal." He turned, his gaze following her as she made her way toward the huge bed and fell back on it. A little laugh escaped her lips as she turned onto her side and patted the comforter.

"Come feel how soft this is."

A wide smile spread across his face and he ran toward her, leaping on the bed and landing on his side. She bounced with the mattress and laughed again.

"This place is so much nicer than what I have in the bunkhouse. I can't believe they're giving it to us for free this week. It's crazy. I bet they could be making so much more money if they had paying customers."

He turned onto his back and stared at the ceiling. "It's a numbers game, Kate. They want more people to come here on vacation so they do stuff like have those journalists write the article to highlight them. Advertising. That's all it is."

That was what they needed to do when they got back to Hickory Hollow. As much as he loved the dressage and shows for people who knew how to train well-behaved horses, he'd always wanted to go bigger. But his mother refused to let him join the rodeo.

So maybe he wouldn't bring up the rodeo. He'd pitch the idea of a dude ranch like Silverstone. He smiled, lacing his fingers behind his head. Anything to get rid of the mundane.

He sat up on the bed and glanced over at Kate. "Since we're supposed to be married, I guess we should talk about how to act around each other."

Her eyes seemed to cloud over and she straightened to sit on the bed with her legs crossed. "Yeah. I don't think you thought that one through all the way."

Houston gave her a chagrined smile. "Yeah. I guess not. So, that means hand-holding and maybe a few kisses. Do you think you can do that?"

She lifted her shoulder. "I don't mind you touching me, Houston. I just don't like being put on the spot." Kate nibbled on her lower lip. "I don't like feeling like an animal at the zoo."

"I don't think people are going to be paying much attention to you specifically. They're all here for the same reason. But I understand what you're saying." He slapped his hands on his legs and got to his feet. "Well, good. Then we're set to do just the basics. There won't be any confusion if we set clear guidelines. So, what's it gonna be? A ride or the gardens?"

She cocked her head slightly and her eyes lit up. "I want to see the gardens. I see horses every day. And like you said, we'll be going for a ride a little later."

CHAPTER SIX

KATE MET HOUSTON'S EYES ACROSS THE BENCH ON THE carriage. No one was waiting for the carriage when they showed up to take a ride over to the hotel property, so it was just the two of them. Well, and the driver. But he probably couldn't care less whether they were supposed to be there. If they let slip that they were imposters, the guy wouldn't think much of it. At least, that was how it felt.

She leaned in closer to Houston. "I've never been on a carriage ride like this before."

He placed his hand on her knee and patted it. "For the next few days, you're going to do all the stuff you've never done before. And more." He gave her the special little smile that had always been reserved for her and consequently made the girls he was dating jealous.

She didn't know why. He had a smile that was just for them, too. But this one was one he reserved just for her and Georgia, one that made her know he cared about her.

He'd always been so sweet and protective of the two of them. And she had counted herself lucky for it.

They bumped over a section of trail and she was nudged closer to him. When he slipped his arm around her shoulder, the warmth of his body made the hairs on her arms raise. Her stomach flipped unexpectedly. That was strange.

They went over another bump, which caused her stomach to flip once more.

Okay, that made more sense.

They passed shrubbery and natural wildflowers on their way toward a large hotel that towered in the distance. Houston had been right about this place. It was huge, and it drew thousands of people on a weekly basis. For the life of her, she couldn't understand why he would want to bring crowds like this to Hickory Hollow. It was perfect the way it was. They had their own little retreat, their own little piece of paradise. They didn't need anything more.

She sighed. But then, what did she know? Houston was going to run Hickory Hollow one day. Maybe he had a better sense for these things.

The carriage lurched to a stop and the driver turned toward them. "The last ride will be at nine tonight. Enjoy your visit."

Houston had already climbed down from the carriage and stood on the ground, looking up at her. He smiled as he lifted his hands. "Want me to help you down, *lover*?"

Kate rolled her eyes, placing her hands on his shoulders. His strong fingers wrapped around her waist and he gently lifted her down from the carriage. He turned and set her in front of him, his hands lingering at her sides. She didn't remove hers from his shoulders either, caught off guard by the strange look he was giving her. His eyes had narrowed and he was staring as if she had something on her face.

She wiped at her mouth with the back of her hand. "What? Do I have something?"

He shook his head, releasing her. "Nope." He gave her an unsettling smile right before he pointed toward the sidewalk that led toward the hotel. "How much do you want to bet that we have to head that way?" He brushed past her and strode toward the hotel without checking to see if she was following him.

Kate scurried after him, catching up after a few feet. "Why do you think they built this hotel?"

Houston shot her a look as he shoved his hands into his pockets. "From what I understand, one of the daughters who grew up here fell for a billionaire who does real-estate. So he built this place as a way to expand the ranch."

"Where did you hear that?"

His lips lifted into a sneaky-looking smile. "You can get a lot of information when you're wandering through chatty crowds. People share a lot when they don't realize an outsider is listening."

Kate's brows furrowed. "So, the daughters of that guy all married men they met here, right? And they're all rather famous in their own right?"

Houston shrugged. "I guess."

"But everyone who came for the article—they didn't necessarily meet their romantic interests here. They just fell in love here."

He glanced at her out of the corner of his eye. "Is there something you're getting at?"

"No. Just curious." She folded her arms as they continued walking, and her gaze bounced to him once more. "Did Lucas tell you about their story?"

Houston snorted. "Yeah. It's like everyone around here wants to share their life story."

"I still can't believe they ended up together after Harper left him at the altar. It's like it was destiny."

He slowed his steps as they continued walking down the trail. "Sometimes people need time apart before they can realize they're good together."

"I don't know, Houston. They weren't both supposed to be here at the same time."

This caused him to stop. Kate took a few steps before she realized he was no longer by her side. She turned and gave him a curious look. "What?"

Houston shook his head. "Nothing. That doesn't mean this place is magic. I'm sure if they were meant to be together, the universe would have a way of making it happen."

A wry smile touched her lips as he closed the distance between them. "Maybe the universe picked this place to help people fall in love."

He rolled his eyes. "Any place can be *that* place. Face it, Kate. This place isn't *special*. And I'm still leaning toward all these people being hired to tell these stories."

"If that were true, then don't you think they wouldn't have put out an article asking people to submit their stories?"

Houston's steps slowed again. "I guess that's a good point." Then he shook his head. "Nah, they could have put out the article request to stir up interest. It doesn't have to be legitimate to serve a purpose."

"Okay, then why would they invite *us*? We aren't"—she looked around and dropped her voice to a whisper—"*in love*. Why risk asking for strangers to come at all? It would be a waste of money."

He seemed to be considering her arguments.

She'd had plenty of time to think this over while she'd been hanging back during the opening reception. There might be a few plants in the group of people who mingled at that welcoming social, but not *all* of them would be. The offer of a free weekend getaway was too tempting for people to resist.

A quick glance in his direction confirmed his confidence was wavering. His lips had been pulled down into a frown and his brows matched. "That's only *one* flaw in my—"

Kate gasped as they came up beside an open area filled with shrubbery, vines, and a multitude of flora. Her pace quickened as she strode inside the garden.

"Oh, Houston. Just *look* at it. Compare Silverstone to Hickory Hollow all you want, but we have nothing that even comes close to this."

She hurried down the cobblestone path, deeper and deeper into the garden.

The scents that surrounded her were next level. The spectrum of color put rainbows to shame. She turned around, checking that Houston had followed her inside. He glanced around a few times, but his focus seemed to be more on her than anything else. He had a soft kind of smile on his lips as they wandered farther in.

"Garden" was a term that didn't quite fit this place of wonder. It was more like a labyrinth with surprises around every corner. She stopped to smell a bluebonnet and smiled. The blues in the petals were more vibrant than she'd ever seen.

She glanced at Houston. "Aren't they wonderful?"

He nodded. His hands remained in his pockets as they continued to explore. "I didn't realize you loved flowers so much."

Her brows lifted. "Really?"

Houston shook his head slowly from side to side.

"Well, prepare to be amazed." She pointed to some large yellow flowers. "Those are buttercups and if you hold it up to your chin and it reflects yellow, then you like butter."

He chuckled. "Somehow, I don't believe that."

She snickered. "Yeah, it's just a game I played as a kid." She pointed out a few more flowers then stopped by a cluster of purple flowers. "These are prairie verbenas. There are actually more than three-thousand species of this plant across Texas, and their petals are often used in herbal teas."

Houston's brows creased. "How do you know so much about flowers?"

Kate shrugged, her pace slowing as they turned down a small path where shrubbery rose on either side of them. "I guess it happened when I spent so much time in the library at school. When you don't have a lot of opportunities to hang out with friends, you do what you can to entertain yourself." She tossed him a smile. "I found I had an affinity for remembering plant facts. Well, flowers more than anything else."

Her fingers trailed along the rows of petals as they passed them. "I always thought it would be fun to become an herbalist. But it wasn't really in the cards for me."

"Why not?"

She let out a puff of air between her lips. "I didn't have the money for college. I mean, after my uncle died, your parents helped to provide for me until I could save my own money, but I just wasn't able to make that happen." She paused in front of some yellow flowers. "These are Texas yellow stars. They're my favorite."

He stopped beside her and looked down at the simple plant. The yellow flower had five petals that sprung out at all angles.

Houston glanced at her out of the corner of his eye. "Why do you like them?"

A soft smile touched her lips. "They're part of the sunflower family. But they're so different, you'd never know. They're unique but they still belong."

She gazed at the flower wistfully. It was how she felt as part of the Ripley family. She'd been welcomed by them so easily, and yet she wasn't *really* part of their family—only in name. She was different and yet part of them.

But she'd never say that out loud. She'd be mortified if Houston ever heard her say something like that.

He leaned forward and plucked a flower from its stem.

Kate gasped. "You can't pick the flowers, Houston!"

With deft precision, he brushed her hair away and placed the bloom over her ear. His eyes shifted to meet hers and it was like an electrical current passed between them. His touch sent chills down her spine.

"Why not?" he murmured.

"What?"

Houston gestured around them. "There aren't any signs. No one said we couldn't pick a flower. Why can't I add to your beauty with something that means so much to you?"

Her heart pounded in her chest. Houston had never been so forward before. He was flirting with her like he did with the girls back home. It was—wrong.

She took a step back, itching to pull the flower from her ear and give it back to him. But what good would that do? He wasn't about to put it in his hair.

Houston was just being nice. It was how he showed her he cared. He'd brought her here to help put her at ease.

He jutted his chin down the path they'd been taking. "Do you hear that?"

She craned her neck and closed her eyes. It was soft, like a whisper through the trees, but there it was nevertheless—a gurgling sound. Kate opened her eyes wide and gazed at him with surprise.

"A fountain?" she whispered.

He nodded. "Should we go look for it?"

He held out his hand, much like he would have done when they were children and he wanted her to come along with him somewhere. She stared at his open palm, still unnerved by the strange feelings she'd been experiencing since arriving here.

To decline his offer would be strange. He'd notice. She might as well go along with it.

Kate slipped her hand into his and laced her fingers between his. *Zing.* That was the only way she could describe the little sparks of electricity that seemed to tie her hand to his. She looked up at him. Did he feel the same thing?

But Houston wasn't looking at her. He'd already started walking toward the source of the sound.

"You know, when we get back to Hickory Hollow, maybe we could look into some herbalist classes you could take online."

Kate stiffened. "What?"

"Sure. Why not? I think you'd be good at it. And maybe we could do something with it at the ranch. We grow food for the animals, but there's more we could be using that land for. I'm certain there are some plants that would be beneficial for us, whether for our physical health or mental health. What do you think?

Her words died in her throat. What did she think? She thought the idea sounded fun. But it wasn't *realistic*. A garden of this caliber seemed like it would be too much work and only benefit her. And though Houston meant well, it wasn't like he'd be making any changes to the way the ranch was run these days. It would be decades before he was the one making all those decisions.

She swallowed down the disappointment and forced her voice to sound as nonchalant as she possibly could. "Yeah. Maybe."

CHAPTER SEVEN

How did Houston not know about Kate's talent with flowers? He'd thought he knew her better than that. Then again, it would make sense that there were parts of her life he wasn't privy to. Though he treated her like a sister, she wasn't. She spent a lot of time with his family, but there was also a part of her life that she kept to herself.

He'd been given a glimpse into a new window of her life, and he couldn't deny it fascinated him. In that moment, all her anxiety and awkwardness had slipped away. Her whole body had lit up with an excitement he'd never seen before—and it was *beautiful*. Already, he knew he wanted to see it again.

Houston continued to hold her hand, his thumb trailing over her knuckles absentmindedly. They turned left, then right, and finally curved around until they came to a clearing. There was a small fountain in the center, surrounded by stone seating. The water bubbled and splashed around a horse sculpture.

Together they stood there, staring at the artwork. This hadn't been commissioned by a rancher. Ranchers were practical, at least all the ranchers he'd met. There was a purpose for everything they spent their money on. Despite all the land ranchers had to work, they didn't have extra cash for frivolous things like this.

Kate stood beside him, her mouth hanging open. "Wow," she whispered.

He leaned toward her slightly. "How much do you want to bet this was put here by one of the guys who married a Greene daughter?"

She released his hand and moved toward it. "I don't care who put it here. It's incredible." She got close enough that she could sit on the stone that surrounded the fountain. Her eyes remained locked on it. "I've always believed that the world needs pretty things." She turned to look at him. "I feel like people in general need to have art and entertainment or they just would stop living."

Houston snorted, earning himself a dirty look from Kate. Clearing his throat, he rubbed the back of his neck. "Maybe you have a point." He gestured to the property and the towering hotel visible over the shrubbery wall. "It seems to be working for Silverstone to have stuff like this."

"Of course I'm right. People in general want to have the best of both worlds. We crave the finer things, but we want to experience life on the edge."

His mouth quirked up into a half-grin. "Life on the edge? How so?"

She leaned back, resting her palms on the stone, and turned her face to the sky. Her eyes closed and that small smile touched her lips again. "How many stockbrokers do you think could hack it out at our ranch? How many could mend the fences? How many could break a horse?" She brought her face back to look at him.

Houston huffed. "None."

"Right. But here, they can pretend. They can learn some of the skills needed to live on a ranch, and then they can go back to their cushy lives where everything is as they think it should be."

"I'm assuming you're trying to make another point."

She tilted her head to the side. "You're so against believing that this place could help people fall in love. Well, think of it this way. When people fall in love, usually, there's something going on to trigger them to get closer to each other. People fall in love when they experience hardship or something new and exciting. Dating in and of itself is supposed to be exciting."

Again, Kate was making some dang good points.

She continued. "What's the best part of dating someone new?"

He stared at her, waiting for her to answer her own question. When she didn't right away, he asked, "What?"

Kate laughed. "I haven't dated anyone. I'm asking you because you have the experience. I only have my theories."

"Wait, you haven't dated anyone before?" He could have sworn she had. Hadn't she dated someone in high school?

"Don't get off topic. What's the best part of dating someone new?" Kate's teasing eyes warmed him throughout as he continued to stare at her. "Well?"

He considered. "Getting to know them. That first kiss. That first touch."

Her smile widened. "That's what I was thinking. So, when you're starting a new relationship, you look forward to experiencing all those new things with someone." She lifted her hands and glanced around. "Here, they give you all new experiences—things you might not have been able to participate in otherwise. And when you do it with someone for the first time, you're sharing it with them. What if that the biggest reason people are falling in love here? It's like this place has this little bubble. Maybe it's not magic, but it's got all the perfect ingredients to make love happen."

"If that's the case, then we should definitely be able to debunk all of this. We can claim that people are just going through the same things they'd be doing at any theme park."

Kate shrugged. "Maybe. And maybe it *is* magic." She laughed, her eyes now on what he assumed was a very disgruntled look on his face.

"We're supposed to be showing everyone that this place is a complete lie. Do you or do you not believe that this place is making people fall in love?" Houston remained in his place, watching her as she seemed to be choosing her words.

"I think…" Her eyes lifted to meet his. "I think that magic doesn't exist as much as I would like it to. I think this place is primed to help people find love because of human nature. But…" She chewed on her lower lip. "But I *don't* think you should be trying to humiliate the people who run this place."

He scoffed. "I'm not trying to humiliate them."

"You're trying to out them as liars."

Houston opened his mouth and held up his finger. He *was* trying to prove that Silverstone wasn't some hot spot for love. But he wouldn't go so far as to say that he was trying to humiliate anyone. "It's the principle of the thing, Kate. They can't claim to be a place where people fall in love when it can't be proven."

She stood up from her place and wandered toward him. "What if you fell in love while you were here?"

Warmth spread through his face and settled in his ears. He huffed and folded his arms. "With whom, exactly? You? Because that's never going to happen. And everyone believes that I'm already married. I highly doubt that some random girl is going to bump into me and realize that I'm her soul mate." He laughed, but the sound was more strained than he'd expected it to be.

Kate lifted a shoulder. "I dunno, Houston. This place has all the makings of being just what you claim it isn't. Love can happen when you least expect it. Why don't you get to know the other people here and listen to their stories? Maybe you'll find that they're telling the truth after all."

She brushed past him, heading back down the path they'd come.

She wasn't right. She couldn't be. Silverstone was a glorified theme park.

But why did he have to make so many good points? How had Kate gotten to be so smart?

He chased after her. "I fail to see how getting to know everyone is going to help matters. Like I said, the whole point of coming is to make those columnists write a retraction about this place. Then we can tell them that there are several ranches in Texas people can visit to get the same kind of experience."

Kate shook her head. "I don't understand why you're so determined in pulling attention to Hickory Hollow."

"This isn't about Hickory Hollow."

"Really? Because that's all you keep saying. You want to inform people about other ranches, more specifically, Hickory Hollow. What happened to *helping* people? I thought you wanted to come out here and prove people are not falling in love here and they shouldn't set their hopes too high."

"I am—"

She stopped and spun around. "You convinced me to come here because you wanted to help people, but honestly, I don't see any of that."

The coloring in her eyes seemed to have changed. They weren't warm or excited anymore. They were annoyed. What happened?

She frowned at him and heaved a sigh. "I didn't mind coming out here when it was to help other people learn the truth. But I've been on this property for only a few hours and even I can tell there's something different about it. You can practically feel the earth humming."

His features pinched. "The earth is *humming*?"

Kate's cheeks reddened. "Don't make fun of me. I'm not going to play your little game. You do what you want, but I'm going to enjoy myself here." She turned on her heel and continued on her way out of the gardens. "Dinner is in about an hour. I'll see you there."

He stopped in his tracks. She was leaving him to—what? Did she actually expect her little tantrum to change his mind?

Silverstone wasn't the hotbed for romance everyone was making it out to be.

They exited the gardens and Houston watched her escape down the sidewalk toward the carriage rides. Why did he suddenly feel so alone? He couldn't remember the last time he'd experienced this sort of feeling. His chest hurt a little and it felt like he couldn't breathe.

It was ridiculous.

Houston spun around and headed toward the hotel. If Kate didn't want to help him do what she'd agreed to do, he'd figure it out on his own. And despite what she thought were his motives, she was wrong. He still wanted to help people. But if he figured out a way to make Hickory Hollow a place people talked about, all the better.

HOVERING OUTSIDE THE CAFETERIA, Houston looked down at his watch. Dinner was in about five minutes and he hadn't seen Kate yet. She hadn't been at their cabin, nor was she inside. It wasn't like she would have driven home. Besides, he had the keys to his truck.

He paced outside of the building. If she didn't show up in the next few minutes, he'd leave and just call her. Their last interaction hadn't been great, but it wasn't exactly a fight, either. Unless it was? He'd never been in a fight with Kate. Usually when he got in an argument with Georgia, there were fireworks—like he could literally see sparks shooting from his sister's eyes. It was their genetics. Both their father and mother were hot-headed.

Irritation stirred in his stomach the longer he paced. Other couples had arrived and were moving past him to get into the cafeteria. Where was she? They were supposed to be putting on a show, weren't they? This was half of their plan. What if someone noticed they weren't spending time together? Or worse—what if they thought the two of them were no longer enjoying marital bliss?

He forced a smile at a couple who headed past him. That did it. Kate had said she was going to be here. She needed to abide by her side of things.

He stalked toward the path that led to the cottages before skidding to a stop. Just in front of him, Kate had wandered out of the barn with two people, a cowboy and probably his wife.

All three of them looked happy to be here.

As if Kate could sense his eyes on her, she lifted her focus to meet his. The irritation evaporated just like that. Kate had changed. She wore a fitted yellow sundress that matched the flower she still wore over her ear. Somehow, she'd managed to curl the ends of her pixie cut. Her cheeks were pink and she smiled at him as she drew nearer.

The trio stopped in front of him, and Kate gestured toward the man. "This is August." She shifted her attention to the woman. "And this is Millie. August works here."

Houston's brows lifted. "You *work* here and you're being interviewed? Isn't that, like, a conflict of interest?"

Kate sighed, rolling her eyes. It was small, but he'd noticed it.

"Actually, we're not—"

Quickly, he forced out a laugh. "Kidding."

"August and Millie aren't going to be part of the article. But they get to be part of the festivities just like Ben and his daughters do." Kate glanced at her two new friends. "It was nice to meet you."

August and Millie echoed the sentiment before they took one another by the hand and headed toward the cafeteria.

Houston turned to watch them disappear before he looked back at Kate. His eyes swept over her outfit, all previous annoyance gone. "You look... nice."

The coloring in her cheeks deepened and she looked down at her feet. "Thanks. Millie insisted."

"Really? You seem to be getting along with a lot of people lately. What happened to your anxiety about being around new people?" The embarrassment on her face made him nch. He sho ldn't have pointed it out. "I mean—"

She shook h r head. "It's ne. I was wandering through the barn anc Millie showec up. We got to talking, and yes, during the hole thing, I elt like I was on the verge of having a he t attack." Kat placed both her hands on her cheeks and ook her hea "I don't know what's wrong with me."

He reached ut and snat ed her wrists, pulling them from her fac "Nothing is rong with you."

Her soft br vn eyes lifte to meet his and she smiled. "Thanks, bu ou don't hav to say that just because—"

"I'm not sa g it for any eason other than to help you understand at you're gre just the way you are."

CHAPTER EIGHT

OKAY. SHE WAS BEGINNING TO SEE JUST WHAT ALL THOSE girls in high school loved about Houston. He had a nasty habit of saying the perfect thing even when he had just put his foot in his mouth.

She'd spent the better part of the last hour trying to convince herself that she'd be able to make it through this weekend without him. Some of the stuff he'd been saying was really getting to her, and she was quickly realizing that her opinions differed from his far more than she'd anticipated.

Their views were like vinegar and oil. Sure, they could shake them up together and they might be good in small doses, but if Houston continued bringing up how much he wanted to change Hickory Hollow, she didn't think she'd be able to stomach it.

Hickory Hollow was her home, and it was perfect. No one wanted to live at a theme park for their whole life—okay, some people who were obsessed with princesses might want to, but not her. Kate would rather have an escape from the world.

The garden on the premises was the only thing that she envied. Maybe when they got back to Hickory Hollow, she'd talk with Dakota about growing a small box garden outside her quarters. That shouldn't be too much of a nuisance.

"Kate? You okay?"

She jumped, finding Houston's eyes still locked on hers. She blinked a few times and nodded, the heat in her face getting worse by the second. "Sorry, I was just thinking."

Houston cocked his head to the side and his eyes narrowed. "About what?"

She shrugged. "Stuff." Gesturing toward the cafeteria, she forced a smile and swallowed hard. "You want to go get some food? I hear there will be a dance, too. Apparently, that's something they like to do for opening night."

"You sure? I thought you hated busy places with lots of people."

She grimaced. "I do. I just thought I'd try to be a little more—you know—*normal.*" Her eyes dropped to the ground, but he lifted her chin, forcing her to look at him.

"You don't have to do anything you don't want to do. I really thought when you agreed to come that you'd enjoy yourself here." He searched her eyes. "I'll try to be a little better about that."

Kate nodded. "I appreciate that."

He held out his arm and she slipped her hand into the crook of his elbow. He placed his hand over hers and they headed toward the doors. Music was already playing, and she could smell dinner. They stepped over the threshold and immediately, her anxiety level went through the roof.

Why did this always have to happen to her? Just once, she wished she could participate with people and not feel like an alien. Houston's hand tightened over hers and she looked over to find him offering her a reassuring smile.

"How about we just get a plate and go outside to eat?"

She gave a short shake of her head. "I can do this," she murmured. "I'll be fine."

He nodded and she tried to ignore the concern in his eyes. Houston led her to a table in the far reaches of the room, away from most of the traffic. He pulled out a chair and gestured for her to take a seat.

Kate glanced over at the buffet table where most of the people stood in line, visiting before they served themselves. Her heart beat a little faster. Maybe she'd wait until the crowd died down.

Houston placed his hand on her shoulder and gave it a gentle squeeze. "I'll get us some food."

Appreciation swelled within her and she mouthed the words "thank you." Houston squeezed her shoulder once more and that tingle swept down her spine. She watched him wander between tables and dart around groups of people until he came to the food line. He turned, finding her gaze, and flashed her a smile.

The pattern of her heart increased again and she looked down at her hands. She'd never thought about Houston as being someone she could date. She never thought she'd date anyone really, but definitely not Houston. He was far too confident to settle for a girl like her.

What was she thinking? Houston was like a brother to her. She shouldn't be entertaining thoughts of what a relationship with Houston would be like. That wasn't healthy, was it? Her face warmed at the thought. Thank goodness no one could read her mind right now, otherwise they'd be judging her for more than her anxiety.

A chair beside her was pulled out from the table and someone sat down. Kate stiffened until she glanced over and found Avery. A soft laugh mingled with a sigh escaped her lips. "Hi, Avery."

Her new friend smiled as her eyes swept over the room. "I bet this is a lot, huh?"

Kate shifted in her seat. "It's not so bad. Houston is pretty good at helping."

Avery smiled, her gaze landing on Houston. "I can see that. You two must really be in love."

Kate bit back a laugh. Yes, she loved Houston, but not in the way Avery had assumed. Kate's focus shifted from Houston to Avery. "Yeah. He's great." She racked her brain for what Avery had said about her boyfriend—fiancé? It didn't matter. "Logan seems like a good fit for you, too."

Avery laughed—she actually tossed her head back and laughed. She set her very blue eyes on Kate and shook her head. "You wouldn't have thought it from the way we treated each other when we first met. Oh boy, did we butt heads. It was pretty awful." She set loving eyes on Logan, who was on the other side of the room chatting with someone else. "But yes, we're a good fit—now." She winked at Kate. "What it really comes down to is that you offer something the other person lacks. But I don't have to tell you that, do I?" She nudged Kate with her elbow.

Kate looked over at Houston, who was now staring at them, curiosity burning in his gaze. She shook her head. "Nope, you don't."

There was a sort of yin and yang between her and Houston that she hadn't noticed before. They might be fake married right now, but she couldn't help but wonder what it would be like if Houston saw her the way Logan saw Avery. What would it be like if he wanted more? Treated her like more than just a friend?

Her lips tingled and her whole body heated. She shifted in her seat. These thoughts were foreign and bordered on taboo. There was no reason for her to be thinking about Houston in this way. Heck, he'd probably be disgusted with the course her mind had taken.

Avery continued to chat about various things, as if she'd taken it upon herself to keep Kate at ease. But the more she talked, the more Kate couldn't avoid fantasizing about a different life. Her fingers lifted to her hair, and she fiddled with it. Houston never went for girls with short hair, but she kept it cropped to keep it out of her face.

Her fingertips brushed against the flower and a soft smile touched her lips. He really was very sweet—and a good man despite some of the issues they didn't agree on. But from what she understood life would be very dull if she were to find someone who was just like her.

Houston returned to the table and placed a plate in front of her before he took the seat on her other side. He offered Avery a smile but didn't say anything as he settled into his seat.

Avery gave her goodbye and wandered off.

He leaned close enough for Kate to smell his familiar cologne. "That was the lady you were talking to at that first get-together, right?"

Kate picked up her roll and tore it in half, forcing herself to ignore his proximity. She nodded and picked at the bread. "Avery. She's really nice."

He smiled. "I'm glad you're finding people you get along with." His arm rubbed against hers as he picked up his fork and scooped up some potatoes. "You're right. There's going to be a dance. Do you really want to stay for it?"

His voice sounded unsure, and he glanced at her out of the corner of his eye.

That strange feeling of longing filled her chest once more. If they stayed for the dance, she'd end up being held in Houston's arms. Heat filled her stomach. As much as she would like to pretend that they were a couple, the second they went home, the cold, hard truth of their relationship would return. Staying for the dance seemed like a very bad idea.

Kate stirred her food around on her plate, no longer having an appetite. She lifted her shoulders and dropped them. "I guess we could leave after dinner if you want to."

"Hey," he nudged her with his shoulder, "if you want to stay, we can stay—for as long or short as you want."

Her brow creased and she turned toward him. Why was he going out of his way to treat her nice? She must have had a strange look on her face because he stopped, his fork hanging in midair.

"What?"

"Why are you being so nice?" She blurted it before she had a chance to restrain herself. The blush was already there, and it probably darkened so badly that she must have resembled a ripe tomato.

Houston's mouth fell open. Then, he broke the tension with a laugh. "What kind of question is that?"

"It's just that… we're friends, and you're treating me like we're… more." And in that one sentence, everything went from okay to worse. She shouldn't have mentioned it.

Because his face went slack. He put his fork down on his plate.

What could possibly be going through his head? If he wasn't already treating her differently, he would definitely be changing the way he treated her now. She swallowed around the lump in her throat but it didn't do any good. Shaking her head, she jumped from her chair and attempted to walk away but he grabbed onto her wrist, preventing her escape.

Kate stared down at him, finding his serious gaze on her. He tugged on her hand.

"Look, Houston. I don't know what's gotten into me. Maybe it's the heat or something else. But I shouldn't have said anything."

He released her hand. The smile he plastered on his face didn't look genuine. He was still confused, she could see it written all over his face. Kate took a deep breath and scurried off. She needed some fresh air and she needed it now.

Maybe this ranch really was magic. What else could explain the way she'd suddenly been thinking about Houston in the most absurd ways? They'd spent more than enough time together. If she *really* thought about it, he wasn't treating her any differently than he always had. They were just in a new environment. Anything new could be explained away by his acting around her in public.

He was putting on a show. That was all. And that was all it would ever be.

CHAPTER NINE

WAS HE TREATING HER DIFFERENTLY? HE HADN'T THOUGHT so. Houston went over every interaction they'd had since they arrived. He couldn't think of one instance where she might think he was attracted to her.

Then again, those thoughts had slowly been creeping into his subconscious—like when she'd shown up in that yellow dress. Before now, he'd never seen her in a dress. He'd never combined the idea of femininity with Kate —ever.

But boy, was he wrong. She was every bit as feminine as the women he'd dated when he was in high school and even as he dated on and off in his mid-twenties.

Houston's chest tightened as his eyes followed Kate. She made a beeline straight for the door, leaving him alone once again. Maybe she was right. He'd offered to get her food. He'd even touched her more while they'd been here. But that was purely to help her get settled, right?

Except he'd enjoyed the little moments when they brushed up against each other. And he'd really wanted her to say she was up for staying for the dance. He couldn't deny how much he wanted to do that.

He gave a sharp shake of his head. She didn't want any of that. Wasn't that what she'd just said as she escaped from him? She didn't want him to treat her like they were something more. But they had to for the benefit of everyone here.

Everyone here.

Houston's eyes swept through the room. Shoot. Had anyone noticed the fact that his wife had just stormed out of the room? Should he go after her so the others didn't think the two of them were in a fight?

He shot out of his seat, abandoning his food, and strode after her. As far as anyone was concerned, they were fine. She needed her and he was going to check on her. Yes, that made sense.

Houston passed by a cluster of people, not meeting any of their gazes as he made it to the door. The glare of the late sunlight hit him square in the face. He flinched and held up his hand to shield his eyes. First things first. He needed to talk with Kate.

He didn't see her immediately when he arrived outside, but a flash of yellow finally caught his attention. Kate was headed for the barn. Of course, she'd go in that direction.

She loved the barn back home and spent most of her spare time with the horses. It would be a place of solitude for her.

Jumping off the small porch from the cafeteria, Houston hit the ground running. He darted across the property, making it to the barn after she'd already disappeared inside. She was faster than she looked.

Slowing his steps, he had to wait for his eyes to adjust to the shadows of the structure. About halfway down the aisle, Kate rested against a post that supported the barn. Her hands gripped the sides of it and her eyes were shut. Her chest heaved with each breath she took.

Houston slipped inside and made his way toward her, not wanting to spook her if she needed time to acclimate. Once he was about ten feet away, he cleared his throat.

Kate jumped, a gasp tearing from her throat as her head whipped up and around to face him.

He let out a little chuckle. "You okay?" He took another step toward her and thumbed over his shoulder toward the exit. "What you said back there—"

She stiffened. "I shouldn't have said it. I was being ridiculous. It's fine. I'm fine."

Houston laughed again. "Kate, whatever you're dealing with, you can tell me."

Was it bad that he sort of hoped Kate would admit she wanted something more? Not that he wanted that. But the question of *what if* seemed to be running a marathon in his head. What was the worst that could happen?

He took another step toward her, studying her for any reaction. She looked down at the ground.

"It's just that we have this comfortable relationship. We know where we stand. I don't want to mess that up."

"Mess it up? How would me treating you a little different mess anything up?" It was a legitimate question. "I'm not asking you to marry me."

She flushed and looked down. Okay, so he was close. She may be avoiding this conversation, but based on her reaction, she was concerned about something *more* than their friendship changing.

"Hey," he paused, waiting for her to look up at him, "you and I are close. We know each other pretty well, right?"

Kate nodded.

"Well, hypothetically speaking, if we let something happen between us while we're here and it doesn't work out, would you up and move away? Would you refuse to set foot in my house?"

"I-I don't know." Her eyes were wide, almost like she was a deer staring into a pair of headlights. "I've never dated anyone before. I mean, I've never even been kissed."

He blinked. That couldn't be possible. She might be shyer than the average girl. "Surely you've kissed a boy."

The scarlet hue of her face said otherwise. She looked away. "Don't laugh at me, Houston."

"I'm not. I just—wow. I guess I haven't been paying as much attention as I thought I was."

Slowly, she brought her gaze back to meet his. "What is that supposed to mean?"

"I could have sworn you've been on dates with guys."

Kate shook her head.

He closed the distance between them. "Maybe we need to change that."

Her mouth formed a perfect little 'o' and, if possible, her eyes widened further. "What?" She shook her head. "No. You don't have to do that. I don't need—"

"Do you even know what I'm offering?" One side of his mouth quirked up into a half-smile.

She shook her head, but no words escaped her lips.

He stood in front of her now. It would be easy to pin her to the post she leaned against. His gaze dipped to her lips. "I'm not necessarily suggesting we date."

"You-you're *not*?"

He didn't miss the tension and disappointment in her voice, which caused his smile to widen. "I'm not."

Her voice cracked. "Then what *are* you suggesting?"

Houston placed his hand against her cheek and brushed the pad of his thumb across the smooth, warm skin of her cheek. "A kiss."

She sucked in a sharp breath and her chest rose and fell a little faster.

"Would that be okay?"

Lifting his focus to her eyes, he studied her. He wasn't about to force her to do anything that would mess with the trust they had developed over the years. Still, a small part of him coul n't deny just now much he wanted her to consent to a ss. Her full, p nk lips parted.

Would it be bad if he cr ssed that line? There could be consequence he wasn't co sidering at the moment. But if he were ho st, he didn't ally want to think about that right now.

Kate had ne r been kissed

He lowered is voice and t came out more husky than before. "Wh better way experience a kiss than with someone yo care about? ur first kiss should be tender but at the s ne time so f led by desire that you don't want it to en "

She was stil rozen, but he eyes shifted to his mouth. She moistened h r lips. "And ou want to give that to me?" Her timid re onse caused is stomach to flip over.

Houston se ched her ga , almost pleading with her admit she w ited this as m ch as he did.

Laughter e pted, and ey both jumped. Houston swiveled his ead toward t e entrance to the barn to find a couple head g their way. Dang it. There went his shot. She had bee so close to tel ng him she wanted him to kiss her. He coul feel it. But th appearance of the couple shattered any in nacy that had een created between them.

He turned b k toward Ka to find the post she had been leaning agai t empty. He j mped and spun around to see her heading own the opp ite side of the barn. There was a small doo hat led out in o the evening air and she was moving *fast*.

Without much thought, he charged after her. This conversation wasn't over. By the time he made it to the door, she was already outside and about to turn the corner of the building. He jogged in that direction.

"Kate!" he called.

Either she didn't hear him, or she was ignoring him. *Great.* He'd mis-stepped. He'd darted after a skittish rabbit. Of course she would leap off into the bushes to get away from him. She was scared.

Houston made it around the side of the barn and came skidding to a halt. Kate was leaning against the side of the barn, her breathing short and ragged. Her face was bright red and when she looked at him her eyes flashed with something foreign.

She nodded, and the word came out with a puff of air: "Okay."

"Okay?" Slowly, he approached her, but the action felt more like he was stalking her rather than helping her not to be so scared. "Okay, what?"

Kate squeezed her eyes shut. "I want you to kiss me."

He stopped two feet in front of her. "Are you sure?"

Her eyes opened and she peeked at him. "I have to get it over and done with at some point. It might as well be with someone I like."

Tilting his head to the side, Houston fought the little voice in his head that practically shouted this was a bad idea. Why would this be bad? He was helping a friend. That was all. They'd both made it clear they weren't ready to date each other. This was just for fun.

So why was his heart hammering and his pulse racing?

Because he actually wanted this. That much was clear. Houston moved close enough their bodies were nearly touching. He set a steady gaze on her.

"I just want to make certain we're on the same page. This is a kiss. That's it. It's not going to be something that turns into more."

She shook her head, then nodded. "Right. This is just a kiss. As far as I'm concerned, it's to help me get past that wall I've been hiding behind."

He bit back a smile, for fear she would take it the wrong way. She was obviously so nervous about the whole thing but trying to come off as confident.

"You're sure this is what you want?"

For the first time since they'd started this conversation, her features went flat. Her jaw was set. Kate shook out her hands and muttered, "Just kiss me, Houston."

Slipping his hand around the back of her neck, Houston pulled her against him. He cradled her in his arms, closed his eyes, and ducked his head. His lips brushed against hers, softly at first, barely touching her.

Kate raised her hands and draped them around him, her fingers threading through the hair at the back of his head. Her touch was soft, teasing, and set off a string of sensations through him he wasn't prepared for. Sparks of electricity shot down his spine, making his extremities tingle with something he'd never experienced before.

And just like that, she released him, pulling away from him.

Houston blinked, his hands dropping to his sides as he stared at her, a cloud of desire still fogging his focus. What had just happened?

He dragged a hand down his face before turning his gaze on her to see if she'd felt it, too.

Kate was staring at the ground, her arms wrapped around her midsection. Uh oh. That wasn't good. No one had had that reaction to him after he'd kissed them. He was a good kisser.

But apparently not good enough.

He cleared his throat and her head snapped up. Her eyes were guarded and her lips were pressed tightly together. What should he say? *Speak, dang it*!

She gestured toward the other side of the barn. "I guess we could go back to the dance, if you want. I think I'd like to watch everyone for a little while."

Or she didn't want to be alone with him. His stomach dropped to his knees. He hadn't expected to feel something so strong when he kissed her.

And now, he'd ruined everything.

CHAPTER TEN

KATE HAD RUINED EVERYTHING. SHE SHOULD HAVE NEVER told him to kiss her. She should have kept running—all the way back to the cottage. If she had made it there before Houston, she could have pretended to be asleep. Then he wouldn't have been able to talk to her until morning.

But now her lips zinged with some kind of electricity she'd never dreamed she'd feel. It wasn't static electricity. That kind of spark was something she'd experienced plenty of times before.

This, this was different.

Her skin hummed with it, singing and doing a dance. She felt like she was back in high school and the boy she had a crush on had just asked her out on their first date. He needed to leave so she could analyze the meaning of everything he had said and done.

But she knew what this meant. It meant *nothing*. He had made that perfectly clear.

The way he was staring at her, he looked almost disappointed. Dang it. Was she supposed to tell him it was good?

She couldn't do that. If she did, she'd reveal everything that was brewing inside her. She had to keep this a secret —a secret she'd take with her to the grave. And there was no way she'd tell Georgia.

Georgia! What would she think if she ever found out? Kate's entire body burned with embarrassment. How could she have kissed Houston? That was such a dumb thing to do!

Houston still stared at her. Even after she'd requested they return to the dance. Was she such a bad kisser that he didn't want to go anywhere with her? That seemed to make the whole situation that much worse.

She swallowed at the hard lump in her throat and turned on her heel. "I'm going. You can come if you want. Or stay here. I don't care."

Kate felt like stomping away. But instead, she focused on keeping her hands clasped in front of her as she wandered back toward the cafeteria. She wouldn't show him how much his kiss had affected her. That would be a death sentence.

Her breathing came out ragged, and her heart raced so fast she didn't know if she would make it to the cafeteria without passing out. Maybe she should sit down on the steps for a little and catch her breath.

Houston's footsteps sounded behind her, but they were slow, almost measured. She couldn't tell if he was upset. It was like he no longer trusted her. The walls he'd pulled up around him made her feel more alone than she had been to begin with.

Whatever. He'd been the one to ask her in the first place. It wasn't like she'd begged him to kiss her. Not really. He'd been the one teasing her and making *her* feel like the dumb one for having never been kissed.

Well, that had changed.

She strode up the stairs toward the entrance to the cafeteria and stepped into the room. Despite the doors being wide open, it was much warmer where everyone visited than it was outside. She slid along the wall until she found a place where she could lean against it in peace and watch everyone. They all looked so happy—and in love.

That was one thing that she'd noticed right off the bat at that first meeting.

Every single person there seemed so *happy*. It was like they'd found the one thing their lives had been missing.

But that couldn't be the same for everyone. People sought different things all the time. Some people wanted money. Others wanted the perfect job. She even knew people who valued travel or buying the next big thing. The only thing these people had in common was that they had found the person they loved. And they'd found them here, at this ranch.

A string of jealousy slithered through her, followed promptly by guilt. She shouldn't be jealous that these people found their true happily-ever-afters. Her life was far from being over. She'd find someone to love—one day.

"They look pretty happy, huh?"

She jumped, a gasp ripping from her throat as she turned to find Houston leaning against the wall with her. She eyed him, waiting for him to make some snide comment about them being more interested in a lie than actually being in love. But he didn't.

Kate turned her attention back to the crowd of people dancing in the middle of the room. "I hear that happens when you fall in love."

He shrugged. "I guess I wouldn't know."

She turned toward him again. "You've never been in love?"

Houston didn't look at her. His focus remained on the people they observed.

"Not enough to ask them to spend the rest of their life with me." His brows pulled together. "I mean, how would someone even *know* something like that?"

When his head turned and he finally met her gaze, a chill rippled through her body.

His gray eyes were so like his twin's. She'd always admired the way they could shift and change with his mood like storm clouds. Right now, they seemed a little darker than normal. And they were pinning her to her spot. Wait, had he just asked her a question? She racked her brain for what he'd just said. Oh, right—knowing if someone was in love.

Kate cleared her throat and forced herself to look out at the people. "I guess that's just something you have to experience for yourself. It's like the way you feel about Hickory Hollow, or your family. It's gotta be something you would be willing to lay your life down for."

"But I don't think I care enough about anything to know if I would be willing to do something like that." Houston sighed. "I mean, I guess I love my family." He shifted, peeking at her. "And you."

Her heart leapt into her throat.

"But I can honestly say I have never met a woman I would do that for."

He was silent for a few minutes and the only thing she could hear was the rushing of her blood in her ears and the sound of the music blasting over the speakers. Then he spoke again, his voice so low she wasn't sure she'd heard him right.

"Do you think there might be something wrong with me?"

Kate stilled, then turned to face him. "Why would you even ask that?"

He lifted a shoulder. "Because I don't believe in love the way they do." He gestured toward the crowd. "Obviously, they have found something I haven't. With how old I am, I would have thought that I would have found at least *something* that resembled that kind of love."

"I don't know. I think a love like that has to be cultivated. Some of these people knew each other before coming here, and some met here. But all of them have known each other for quite a bit longer by now."

Kate pointed toward a couple who was slow dancing, The woman rested her head on the man's shoulder while he held her hand in one of his and held her close with the other. They weren't talking, but the woman was smiling. When they turned slightly, they could see that the man had a half-smile on his lips, too.

"Look at them," she said. "That's the kind of love between two best friends. But I think it's more than that."

"More than being friends?"

She nodded. "I think it's trust, too. But also chemistry."

His lips pulled into a crooked grin. "Chemistry?"

She felt the blush seeping beneath her skin before it hit with full force. "Sure. You have to *want* to be in that person's arms. You have yearn to be touched by them, to be with them."

She looked down. It was beginning to feel like she was describing how she felt about the kiss he'd just left her with.

No. She wouldn't allow herself to dwell on the impossible. She was just reeling from her first kiss. All first kisses were probably like that. She wouldn't be lucky enough to find the perfect kind of chemistry with the first guy she let kiss her.

And yet, something told her that it was possible. Rare, but possible.

It was getting harder, but she forced her attention to remain on the people they were watching rather than the man who stood beside her. She needed to stay on her A-game. After this weekend, they would go home and she'd have to forget all about the kiss they'd shared. But maybe she'd be a little less nervous and a little more prepared to really start dating.

Kate placed her hands behind her back and pressed against them. They had begun to shake a bit. This conversation wasn't one she was prepared to have with Houston at the moment.

"You want to dance?"

She stilled and her heart picked up the pace once again. "What?"

A new song had started. But he couldn't possibly be asking her that. They shouldn't be touching, not after what had just transpired between them. She didn't know if she could keep herself from leaning in and kissing him under those circumstances.

Her mouth was dry, like her tongue had turned into sandpaper. Water. She needed water.

Houston rolled his eyes, reached out, and grabbed her hand. "It's not like I'm going to kiss you again. Been there, done that."

If she wasn't so anxious, she might have laughed as he pulled her onto the dance floor. That was *exactly* what she was worried about. But not for the reasons he was probably thinking.

Rather than keeping her right hand in his left, he placed both hands on her waist, allowing her to get even closer than she'd expected. His scent was intoxicating. It had never been something she'd paid much attention to, but now she was rapidly associating it with the way her stomach clenched and knotted in a rather pleasant way.

Don't look at him. Don't do it or you'll be locked in place again.

She could feel his gaze on her, and it was infuriating and invigorating at the same time. He was only looking at her because he was dancing with her. There wasn't any other reason beyond that. They both knew it. So, it was time to rid herself of these childish thoughts. She could look at him. Nothing would happen.

Kate lifted her gaze to meet his.

Wrong again.

The second their eyes met, memories of their kiss swept through her with the same feeling of adrenaline. Just chemistry.

Just *dang good* chemistry.

She let out an exasperated sigh. This must be what every girl who had a crush on him had felt. And now, she inexplicably found herself in the same boat. Only in her situation, she wasn't allowed to do anything about it—not in the typical sense, anyway. There were more important things than silly crushes.

Houston cocked his head to the side, his brows pinched as he studied her. It was almost like he could see her thoughts. His act filled her face, but she couldn't pull her gaze from him. What was she going to do now?

She'd had enough. Her body was not only exhausted from their trip, but from the emotional strain she'd been through. The day only had twenty-four hours in it, but she felt like she'd been through several days already.

Kate tore herself away from Houston and headed across the dance floor. It took only moments for him to catch up, though he almost had to jog to keep up with her. "Hey, where are you going?"

She glanced at him out of the corner of her eye. "Home."

"Home? You can't drive home this late—"

"Not *home*. Obviously not there. I meant the cabin. I'm tired and I want to go to bed." Once they made it outside, she slowed her steps. "We have a long couple of days, Houston. I would rather be well-rested before we participate with everyone. You'd be wise to do the same. Especially if you're still set on proving that people here aren't really in love."

His mouth opened and closed like some kind of fish, but he didn't argue. Good. Maybe he was beginning to realize what she'd figured out. They couldn't be together even if they wanted to because of their past.

CHAPTER ELEVEN

HOUSTON SAT ON CHAISE LONGUE IN THE BEDROOM. A SOFT glow filtered into the room, landing on the large bed. Specks of dust drifted through the air, glittering against the beam of light they floated through.

He brought his focus over to Kate's sleeping form again. Restless, he itched to get to his feet and pace the floor but doing so would likely wake her up, and that was the last thing he wanted. Kate needed her sleep, and he needed a quiet room.

Last night had been a major surprise. His kiss had gone haywire. For all this talk of love, fake or real, he had been knocked off his feet when his lips had brushed against hers.

Okay, so to think he'd fallen in love with Kate—*that* kind of love—it was ridiculous.

Or was it?

Houston blew out a frustrated breath and pushed both hands through his hair. Whatever had happened, he wanted more. He couldn't stop thinking about it—obsessing over it. Deep down in his bones, he knew this sort of feeling only came around once in a lifetime.

Relationships couldn't just be built on chemistry, though.

Which is why this was so hard.

Because he knew he liked Kate. They got along well. She was practically already part of the family.

Houston shut his eyes and laid back on the chaise again. He pulled the sheet up over his legs and stared at the ceiling. Today, they were supposed to do some skill exercises like roping. Then, they were going on a ride and picnic for lunch. In the evening, they had another romantic dinner planned, but this one was outside under the stars.

Boy, Silverstone knew how to go all out for things like this. Maybe *that* was their trick. They created opportunities for couples to be forced together.

That made a lot of sense. He could tell his parents to do the same. Granted, they didn't have the land size that Silverstone did, but they could still draw people for activities during the day.

Kate rolled over, a soft sigh leaving her lips, but she didn't wake. Her eyes remained closed, her serene face turned so he had the perfect vantage point to watch her sleep.

Thoughts of his ranch disappeared as his gaze dipped down to her mouth. Her soft, full, pink lips curved upward into a smile. She let out another sigh and her arm came up to curl over her head like she was a glorified ballerina. The wisps of hair that framed her face only added to the angelic scene.

A hard lump formed in his throat and he grunted as he turned over onto his side and slammed his fist into his pillow. Thinking about her like this was inappropriate.

Why?

Why was he so against getting close to her? Hadn't he been the one to kiss her? Georgia would have said he was toying with her, but was he, really?

Houston shot up in his spot. He should be looking at this from a different angle. Why not take this opportunity to see if this ranch could really make two people fall in love? His eyes landed on her again. He hadn't really been interested in finding a soul mate before. Kate was as good an option as any, right? And if it didn't work out, it wouldn't be that big of a deal.

He chuckled under his breath. He couldn't believe he was actually considering any of this. But there it was.

HOUSTON LOOKED over at a nearby couple holding hands. These people were *too* in love. No one acted like that all the time. He glanced down at Kate's hand dangling at her side. He could hold her hand and see her reaction. Or maybe he wanted to hold her hand for an entirely different reason.

The tumultuous thoughts in his head continued to battle it out until everything pounded painfully. He needed to stop second-guessing himself. That wasn't something he normally did. The way he interacted with Kate needed to be approached with the same kind of confidence and care he was known for. They were here to pretend to be married, after all. She couldn't turn him down without drawing the attention of the others that surrounded them.

And so what if he had started to feel some level of attraction toward her? That wasn't so bad.

He took in a deep breath and grabbed her hand, bringing it to his lips.

Her wide eyes turned, staring at him in disbelief. But just as quickly as that expression had appeared, it morphed into something unreadable. True to his prediction, she didn't yank her hand from his grasp.

The cowboy from one of their first get-togethers, August, held up a rope and flashed a smile to the group. "The last time you were here, it's likely you had a chance to learn to lasso a cattle bust. But this time is going to be a little different."

He jerked his chin toward the corral behind him.

Houston leaned to his left to get a better look and found a calf wandering along the fence.

August continued, "The men will have a chance to rope the calf. While that's taking place, we'll have the women get a cooking course with our chef."

A smile touched Houston's lips. Kate wasn't going to like that.

As if she read his thoughts, Kate snorted and leaned closer to Houston. "I'm better at roping calves than you and you know it." She met his gaze. "Maybe you should go take the cooking class and leave the hard stuff to the experts."

He chuckled and tugged on her hand to pull her closer to him. "Maybe we should do both of them together."

Her features pinched. "The class is going on while the guys are roping."

Houston's hand shot up, drawing August's attention. He cleared his throat. "I thought this little retreat was for couples. Wouldn't it make more sense to let the women watch their men at work and let the men do the cooking course, too? Isn't that what people are paying for?"

August exchanged a look with his wife then he swung his focus back to the group. "What do you guys think? Want to make this interesting?"

Several of the men whooped and the women cheered.

"Alright. Whoever gets the best time will win another all-expenses paid trip back to Silverstone to celebrate their anniversary." August laughed with the additional cheers that filled the air. He turned to Millie. "Tell Tyson to get some more calves. We're gonna need them."

Houston froze, his eyes following Millie as she hurried toward the barn.

Kate dug her elbow into Houston's side. "You don't think—"

"Didn't Tyson Lee marry some rancher's daughter?" Houston murmured.

Her wide eyes shifted toward the barn where Millie had disappeared. "You're thinking Tyson Lee, the rodeo star, married one of Ben's daughters, too?"

Houston took off his hat, releasing her hand and ran his fingers through his hair. "Well, they have a movie star, a chef, a billionaire, and a prince. There were five daughters, right?"

She nodded. "But that's too much of a coincidence, right?"

"You talking about Tyson?"

Both of them jumped, finding August standing beside them. The cowboy's eyes were narrowed, but he wore a knowing smile on his lips.

"You know, I don't recognize you two. When did you say you attended?"

Houston flashed him a smile. "It was with that wedding a few months back."

August tilted his head. The question still burned in his eyes, but he didn't request additional information. Instead, he glanced toward the barn. "Tyson Lee did marry a Greene girl."

Kate faced August, excitement clear in her face. "He hasn't been in a rodeo for a few years, but I heard he's going to return for one more competition. Is that true?"

The cowboy gestured toward a man approaching them. "Why don't you ask him yourself."

Both Kate and Houston's heads turned as one as a man in his late forties approached, pulling two calves by two separate ropes.

Kate let out a squeal and shot Houston a look. "Do you think he'd sign something for me?"

August patted her shoulder. "I'm sure he'd love to. But we're busy today. You'll have to catch him another time." He strode off, jogging to meet up with Tyson.

Kate whirled around and faced Houston. "Can you believe it?"

Houston shook his head slowly. "I can't," he murmured. This was all too coincidental.

None of it made sense. It was either a big scam or it was the strangest dude ranch ever operated. It was entirely possible that this ranch drew people solely because of all the famous people who resided here. And if that was the case, then Hickory Hollow didn't have a shot at making it on the map.

Kate grabbed his hand, dragging him toward the corral where they had already given three different men each a rope. She didn't release his hand as they stood side by side.

Houston's gaze dropped to where she remained connected to him. And just like that, the disappointment or disillusionment evaporated. Kate was excited to be here. She was enjoying herself and he didn't want to mess that up. It was more important that he step back and observe than actively go after what he'd come here to do.

She met his eyes with a wide grin, and he offered one in turn. It was clear the men who'd gone through the first round didn't know what in the world they were doing.

They could toss the rope, sure, but making it onto the calf's head was a feat they couldn't master.

Someone brought by a lasso for Houston and as he stared at it in his hand, he got the distinct feeling that he shouldn't participate. Kate gave him a confused look, but he just shoved the rope into her hand. "You go."

Her brows lifted and she bit out a laugh. "What?"

"You said so yourself. You're better at this than me. If we want to win, you need to do it for us."

Her fingers wrapped around the coil and her eyes darted to meet his again. "Really?"

Houston's bark of laughter drew the attention of some of the people who were closer to them. He nodded to the corral. "Of course. And if we win and you don't want to come back, we can give the trip to someone else."

The grateful smile that touched her lips warmed him from the inside out. This was exactly what she needed. He could feel it. Kate nodded and hurried toward the corral. She ducked down to slip between the bars of the corral, paused to look at him once more, and stepped into the enclosure.

CHAPTER TWELVE

KATE'S HAND WRAPPED TIGHTLY AROUND THE COIL OF ROPE IN her hand as she stared at the calves now wandering freely in the corral. There were three of them, and one was more timid than the others. It was fast, but once it got roped, it seemed to settle sooner.

The other two were fighters. The last thing she wanted was to get kicked in the stomach while she was hogtying the beast. August entered the corral and opened his mouth to speak, but then his eyes landed on Kate. One side of his mouth lifted and he stepped toward her.

"Do you realize this is a man's event?"

She huffed. "Are you saying I'm not capable of doing it?"

She was in her element. It was like the rope gave her the confidence she lacked in the social events. Right here, right now, in front of others but with the rope in her hand and the dirt beneath her boots, she knew she was right where she was meant to be.

August studied her, amusement in his eyes. "I just assumed you'd want to let your husband do the dirty work. It doesn't seem quite fair to have you be in here—"

"I assure you, I'm far better equipped to handle this event than he is."

She tossed him a look over her shoulder, her stomach flipping pleasantly as she found his eyes watching her. He could have been stubborn and taken this opportunity. But he knew her. That knowledge only made her insides churn more.

Houston was probably the only one who did. He'd been the only one she'd let get close to her. It wasn't any wonder that the more time they spent here, the more curious she'd become over starting a relationship with him —a *real* relationship.

She focused once more on August, lifting her chin. "It shouldn't matter which one of us is going to compete. This activity is couples against couples, right?"

August's eyes flitted from her to Houston and back. He shrugged. "I suppose you're right." He turned, heading back to the center of the corral to prepare this set of contestants.

She bent her knees, pulling the rope loose in her hands so she'd be prepared when August blew the whistle.

The sharp chirp burst in the air and she jolted into action, immediately diving for the calf she knew would be the easiest. The rope in her hand swiveled around, spinning and gaining speed over her head before she released it with a flick of her wrist. The rope flew gracefully onto the calf's neck and she yanked it tightly, digging the heels of her boots into the dirt to stop the animal from bolting.

Her gloved hands deftly pulled the calf closer and she managed to get it onto the ground. Everything around her faded—the cheers, the catcalls, and even the landscape. All she could hear was the sound of her own breathing and the rush of her blood in her ears.

Kate straddled the animal, wrapping the rope around its leg and crossing it to two more to tie them all together. Instinctively, her hands shot in the air.

She looked around the ring, her eyes landing on several shocked faces until they found Houston's proud expression. He gave her a short nod, then blew a whistle with his fingers. That's when Kate noticed the other two men were still trying to secure their animals. One had gotten his on the ground but couldn't get the rope tied around his legs. The other was pulling on his calf, but the stubborn beast wouldn't be urged onto its back.

Tyson stood on the outside of the corral, a funny kind of grin on his face, and August wandered over to her. He chuckled.

"Well, you sure proved me wrong." He held out his hand, pulling her to her feet. "I don't think anyone is going to beat your time. In fact, I don't think the competition was fair at all." He laughed again. "Maybe I can convince Ben to give two prizes for this one. You're one talented cowboy."

Her cheeks warmed at the compliment, and she brushed stray hair from her face. "Thank you."

Kate turned, her eyes landing on Houston again. His eyes didn't leave her face. In fact, the way he stared at her was almost like the way he looked at the girls he was interested in dating. His heart stuttered, stumbling as it attempted to pump the blood to the rest of her body. She'd been so distracted by Houston she didn't notice that August had left to speak to someone else.

Hurrying over to where Houston stood, she slipped between the bars. She threw her arms around him and gave him a tight hug. His arms wrapped around her waist, holding her in place.

She pulled back, grinning like an idiot. "Did you *see* that?"

He laughed. "Yeah. I saw."

Kate placed her hands on her cheeks, letting out a little laugh. She stepped back and bounced on the balls of her feet. "I have never been so in the zone before. I mean, I know I'm better than these other guys," she let out a little squeal, "but that was *amazing*."

When she settled her focus on him again, she stiffened. There was a seriousness in his gaze that made everything inside her run hot and cold all at once.

Houston brought up his hand and placed it against her cheek. "You were fantastic, Kate."

She stilled, warmth having been thrown all over her nervous energy like a weighted blanket. Maybe it was the way his mouth formed those words. Or it could be the timber of his voice. Houston just seemed to have a knack for grounding her back to reality.

Kate offered an embarrassed smile. "Thanks."

As if against her will, her eyes dropped down to his mouth, the memory of their kiss yanked to the forefront of her mind. What if his kiss could mean more? What if they could *be* more?

She couldn't allow herself to dwell on that fantasy. They'd agreed that their kiss didn't mean anything. He'd offered it to her as a way to break the ice for future relationships. But she wasn't so sure she wanted to be in a relationship with anyone else.

"Kate," he murmured, his finger grazing her skin as he brushed aside some hair.

She lifted her eyes to meet his. "Yeah?"

His warm eyes searched hers, full of questions she couldn't decipher. Her heart lurched in her chest. She couldn't dare hope he shared similar thoughts of their kiss.

He moved closer to her, their bodies almost touching. "I wanted to—"

"That was amazing!"

Someone clapped her on the back and Houston's eyes shifted slightly upward behind her. And just like that, a wall was erected between them. He glanced at her then away as he stepped back.

Kate turned to the intrusion, her irritation growing until she met Tyson's eyes. Her stomach bottomed out and her legs went numb. "Tyson Lee?" she squeaked.

He chuckled and held out his hand. "You have a good eye and a talent I haven't seen in some time." Tyson beamed at her. "Have you ever considered competing in the rodeo?"

Chills ran through her body and she choked out the word, "No."

"Well, you should. I watched you. I could tell you had a strategy set up before August even blew that whistle. With natural talent like yours, I'd wager you'd win your fair share of events." He removed his hat and ran a hand through his hair before returning it. "I'm actually looking to put together a team before I retire, and I think you'd be a good fit."

Her eyes widened. *"Really?"* She had never thought about competing in a rodeo before. As far as she was concerned, her life would start and end at Hickory Hollow. But this idea opened up so many possibilities—travel, money, and community.

"I'd have to see what else you're good at, but I think it's safe to say—

Houston's arm slid around her waist and pulled her a little too tightly against his side. "We work at a ranch a few hours from here. We're too busy for rodeos."

Kate stiffened and shot a look at Houston.

Tyson's focus shifted from Kate to Houston. "That's a shame. Well, if you change your mind, reach out."

They watched Tyson wander away. When he was out of earshot, Kate shoved Houston.

"What did you do *that* for?"

"What?" His brows pulled together. He gestured toward where Tyson had disappeared. "Did you really believe him?"

Her mouth dropped open. "You *didn't*?" Heat filled her face. "I thought you—" She shook her head. "I can't believe you did that." She turned on her heel and strode away.

A heavy weight had settled on her, making it hard to breathe. She would have thought Houston would push her toward something exciting like this—support her and be excited for her.

He hadn't even given her a chance to think it over before he told Tyson they weren't interested. It didn't make sense.

Yes, she was her own person, and she had the right to make her own decisions. She could track down Tyson and tell him she was interested all on her own, but where would that leave Dakota and Brady? Houston's parents were practically the only other family she had. If Houston was against this, it wouldn't be too far off to believe that his parents would feel the same way.

Kate strode with quick sure steps, though she had no idea where she was going to go. Their next activity would be in thirty minutes to an hour. If she didn't show up, people would surely notice. And Houston would be furious. He'd brought her here to pretend to be his wife, after all.

But right now, she didn't want to see him. She needed to analyze what she wanted to do with her life. Tyson had opened a door and she wasn't so certain she wanted to shut is just yet.

She found herself wandering into the barn. To her right was a ladder that gave access to the loft overhead. She glanced back at the entrance. No one had followed her inside. Chances were slim that she'd get in trouble for poking around. And she'd get to hide away while she figured a few things out.

Climbing the ladder, she found herself in what looked like a storage area. On the far side was a window that overlooked the ranch. Sticking to the shadows, she watched the group still competing. No one seemed to have noticed she'd left—except Houston

He kept looking over at the barn every few minutes, but he didn't make any indication he would follow her.

Kate took in a deep breath and released it slowly. A swirl of emotions spun in her chest like a tornado. When she'd arrived at Silverstone, she'd been content just to let Houston take the lead. But the more time she spent here, the more she realized that he might not be as smart as she thought him to be—well, in terms of his reasons for coming. Houston was smart. He was strong, and confident, and a hard worker. But there were these little things like his inability to let something go when, in the grand scheme of things, they didn't matter.

Like this whole plan to embarrass Silverstone. It was clear this place was different—not that she'd seen much herself, but by interacting with those who'd come here, Kate could tell.

And then there was a completely different side of Houston that she admired and would follow to the ends of the Earth. His love for his family and the people in his life was undeniable. The way he'd prioritized her comfort level when she felt suffocated by everyone here. How he'd stepped aside to let her compete during the lasso activity.

And the fact that he could center her, ground her with just one look.

Houston was everything she wanted in a husband in spite of some of his shortcomings.

Her throat constricted with that revelation. No one was perfect. She knew that.

She stepped away from the window and settled into a seated position on the floor. Picking up a piece of straw, she spun it between her fingers, letting the tip twirl and blur before her vision. Houston had admitted she'd been really good with the calf. Maybe that was why she was so hurt about him interrupting her conversation with Tyson. It was her choice to tell him no.

The big question was whether she would have.

CHAPTER THIRTEEN

HOUSTON SHOULD GO AFTER HER. SHE'D DISAPPEARED INTO the barn, and she hadn't reappeared. It'd only been about ten minutes but he was getting antsy. Kate wouldn't leave, she couldn't. He had their only way home.

Then again, she could call a car to take her. But it would be an expensive ride home. No one from Hickory Hollow had the time to take four hours out of their day to come get her over some childish argument.

Was it an argument?

His brows furrowed as he went over what had just transpired.

The biggest emotion he'd felt had been some form of unease he couldn't explain. He knew the second Tyson had mentioned a team where he was going with it. Heck, Houston had noticed just how good Kate was, too. He couldn't think of anyone else at Hickory Hollow who could have done better. She did have a clear natural talent, they just didn't do much cattle wrangling out at Hickory Hollow. Their specialties were with horse training.

If Kate had accepted Tyson's offer, there was the possibility she'd move away and he'd never see her again. His stomach roiled at that thought. He couldn't let her walk out of his life.

His whole body tightened, and he looked back at the barn. He hadn't expected to feel so strongly over what Kate wanted to do with her life. It was *her* life, after all. If she wanted to try something new, who was he to stand in her way?

Even as the thought crossed his mind, he knew it would tear him up inside if he never saw her again.

Houston let out a groan. At this point, she was probably furious with him. He didn't want her to accept Tyson's offer, but he would have let her tell the guy.

Okay. That wouldn't have been possible. Not with how his feelings for her had changed and morphed into something... different. He wasn't about to risk her telling him that she'd love to give it a try. How was he supposed to go home after this weekend and not have Kate with him?

Georgia would be furious. His parents would support her because they were good like that. But everyone would miss her. She was part of their family.

Suddenly, his feelings didn't seem so benign. He couldn't fall for her. Allowing himself to do so would open him up to some serious heartache. Even if she didn't join up with the infamous Tyson Lee, she could up and leave at any point. And his life was firmly rooted at Hickory Hollow.

"Everything okay?"

He jumped, his gaze shifting to the source of the voice.

Their cabinmates stood in front of him. Lucas had his arm around Harper's shoulder and the two of them looked at Houston with what could only be concern.

Houston had to fight his rising instinct to scowl at the couple. How would that look? Even if they were faking their whole relationship, he wasn't about to draw more attention to the assumption that there was trouble in paradise. He swallowed back the biting comments that could be so easily thrown at the couple and forced a smile.

"Yep. Everything's great."

Harper shot a look at the barn. "Where did Kate head off to? If she needed to find a bathroom—"

"She just likes spending time with the horses. And she's not too keen on crowds. But it looks like we're wrapping up here, so I should probably go find her." He brushed past his interrogators and shook his head. People needed to stop being so outright nosy.

He jogged toward the barn, holding his hat to his head. He needed to come up with some way to put Kate at ease. He'd promised her that they'd have fun here. That didn't mean he had to let her go off and become some great rodeo star. It just meant he'd have to step carefully.

Houston slowed as he made it to the edge of the barn entrance. He walked into the building and glanced around. There were no other individuals inside, which was both good and bad. No one to witness or overhear anything that could get them in trouble. But if he couldn't find Kate in here, he'd have a bigger problem on his hands.

"Kate," he hissed. "You in here?" He stepped farther inside, peeking into stalls as he went. He came to a stop beside a ladder that led into the loft. His head tilted upward. "Kate."

Her head peered over the edge of the loft floor. He'd expected her to have an angry look on her face but instead, she looked chagrined. Her arms were folded on the floor and she rested her chin on them. "Hey," she murmured.

Houston bit back his smile. "Hey." He put both hands on a rung of the ladder followed by one boot. "I guess I should apologize."

"You guess?"

He climbed up two steps. "I should apologize."

"You should," she confirmed.

Houston climbed up another two steps. "I'm sorry."

"For?"

He shook his head, a grin crossing his face. This was one more reason he liked Kate. She didn't let him push her around when she knew he was wrong. She was easy-going, but when he took things too far, she wasn't afraid to let him know. "I'm sorry I didn't let you tell Tyson no."

She arched a brow and crawled back as he made his way to the top. She sat on the floor, pulling her legs up to her chest with her arms wrapped around them. "Who says I would have said no?"

He shrugged, folding his arms as he remained on the ladder and resting them on the floor. "I guess I figured Hickory Hollow was your home and you wouldn't want to leave it. Besides, the way you are with big crowds… it wasn't your speed."

It was a flimsy excuse for what he'd done, but it made sense.

A ghost of something flickered across her countenance. She worried her lower lip and her gaze darted to the ground. "You're probably right."

His stomach knotted and remorse settled like a giant stone in the pit of it. The disappointment was clear in her voice. Whatever hope or interest she'd had in pursuing a rodeo gig had died with his comment. He lifted his chin and flashed her a small smile.

"But you know what? We could go to some of the smaller local rodeos. I'm sure you could whip right through those guys."

Kate peeked at him. "I don't know. It might be safer to just stick with Hickory Hollow. But maybe you could teach me some stuff about horse training."

He perked up. "That interests you?"

She lifted a shoulder. "If I'm going to stick around at a ranch that specializes in horsemanship, it'd probably be a good idea to learn how to pitch in, right? Do you think Dakota would be okay with that?"

Houston climbed the rest of the way into the loft and sat beside her. "I think my mom would be thrilled. In fact, if it was of any interest to our clients, she'd probably be even more please if one of us learned how to do that thera-peutic stuff.'

Kate rested er cheek on her knees as she gazed at him. "You really think so?"

"I know so." He bumped his shoulder against hers, putting her of balance and forcing her to release her knees to catch herself.

They both chuckled, the tension in the air flitting away like a rain cloud after a storm.

Houston nudged her again. "Let's go do that cooking thing."

He made a face, eliciting another laugh from Kate.

"Come on. I can't be as bad as being shown up by a girl in that corral."

"You're probably right."

They both crawled forward at the same time and his hand landed on hers. She stopped and looked up at him at the same time he met her gaze. The charged tension returned to the air but for a different reason.

She moistened her lips, drawing his attention to them. The kiss they'd shared had been for a good reason, and he'd insisted he wouldn't do it again. Granted, they might have to show some affection in front of other people, but they were completely alone here.

Still, it would be so easy to pull her in for a quick embrace. She was so close, and he could hear how her breathing hitched ever so slightly.

Kate wanted this, too. He could feel it in the hum of electricity that passed between them. He leaned toward her, and she did the same as she closed her eyes.

"Hey! I don't think you're supposed to be up there."

Her eyes flew open and they both looked down the length of the ladder at a stranger that Houston didn't recognize. He murmured out of the corner of his mouth, "Did we meet him?"

"I don't know," she whispered. "Do you think he works here?"

The man stood with his hands on his hips as he peered up at them. "Are you here for a specific event?"

Houston cleared his throat. "Yeah. We're with the couples thing."

The man turned his attention toward the entrance. "Well, they're all heading into the cafeteria building. You don't want to be late."

Houston glanced at Kate and snickered. "We should probably go."

She nodded.

They hurried down the ladder and headed for the entrance just as another man hurried past them. "Your Highness, the queen—"

The first man sighed. "Timothy, I told you while we're here, it's just Nick."

Their conversation faded but the look Kate gave Houston was priceless. Her eyes nearly bugged out of her head and her lips mouthed the words "he's a king."

Houston reached for her hand and tugged her along. "We don't know that," he muttered.

She gave him a pointed look. "You need to stop thinking everyone is lying to you. Besides, it's not like he said he was the king. You heard that other guy say it. This place is literally like a fairytale come to life. How can you not believe any of it by now?"

"We'll see."

Kate tossed back her head and let out a laugh that forced him to join in. Her smile warmed him to his core. "I knew you couldn't be so jaded. You'll see. By the time we leave, you'll believe this place is something special."

"Does that mean you'll invite me to come back here?"

Her brows furrowed. "What do you mean?"

"I'm sure you won that last competition. That's an all-expenses-paid vacation."

The coloring in her cheeks pinked and her hand squeezed his. "Sure. If you have a change of heart, I couldn't think of a better reward than to bring you back here for a second trip."

"Deal."

CHAPTER FOURTEEN

THE CAFETERIA WAS PREPARED WITH SEVERAL PORTABLE stovetops set up on tables. Each couple had been given the ingredients to put together a "romantic" picnic. The catch was that they were on a strict timeline because their horses were getting saddled and prepared for a ride.

Where Kate should be focused on the task at hand, she couldn't seem to keep control of her thoughts. The universe seemed to be attempting to teach her a lesson. It was like she wasn't supposed to get too close to Houston or something.

Maybe it was the ranch. If this place was special enough to pull people together, it was logical to assume that it would be special enough to keep the wrong people apart.

That could be exactly what was happening with them.

From the moment she arrived, she could tell something was different about Silverstone. It was so clear she would have been crazy not to see it. And she'd thought maybe the ranch was pushing her toward Houston.

Initially, she'd dug her heels in and refuted that idea. They were like brother and sister. But at some point, a shift had occurred—allowing her to entertain the idea of him.

Two more near-kiss moments and again she was thrust into a position where she wondered what she should do. At this point, nothing had happened. She could keep Houston at arm's length and when they returned home, everything would be status quo.

And then she'd always wonder "what if."

She let out a groan.

"What's wrong?" Houston glanced over at where she was stirring a few veggies into her quiche mixture. "Did you put too much salt in that?"

Kate pressed her lips into a thin line, fighting the blush that seemed to have taken up permanent residence on her face since their first kiss. "No. I was just thinking."

His eyes bounced from her bowl to her eyes. "But nothing is the matter." It was more of a statement than a question, but she answered anyway.

"No…" she drawled.

He corners of his mouth lifted. "Okay…" he said in the same tone. "But hurry up with that because next we have to dip some strawberries. They need enough time to set before we leave on our ride."

She tilted her head as she watched him stir the melting chocolate in the double boiler. He wore a cheesy apron with the silhouette of a cowboy on a horse and the words "hold your horses" embroidered beneath it.

He seemed to have a knack for cooking. They'd already diced some other fruit, prepped the strawberries, and put together a pasta salad. He'd insisted on doing the chocolate, saying he didn't want to scorch it.

"I didn't know you liked to cook."

Houston snorted. "This? This isn't cooking."

"But you *do* like to cook."

He peeked at her, lifting a shoulder. "Sure, why?"

She pulled the whisk from her bowl and placed it on the counter. Turning toward him, she placed her hands on her hips.

"Houston Shipley. How did I not know you liked to cook? Does Georgia know?"

A brusque huff left his lips. "Do you think I'd *ever* let her know something like that? I'd never hear the end of it. Of course she doesn't know."

"What do you like to cook?"

He shrugged again. "I've dabbled with a few things. Mostly, I like baking."

Kate scrunched her nose and tilted her head. "Baking? Like pastries and stuff?"

Cooking over a grill was one thing, but she couldn't see Houston decorating cookies or anything like that. He was a rugged cowboy. Even just making him wear that apron had been somewhat of a trial.

He continued to gently stir the chocolate before he glanced at her. "Yeah."

"What's your specialty?"

Houston snorted. "My *specialty*? You make it sound like I'm some kind of five-star chef."

"Nah."

He looked up at her, his expression blank.

Kate laughed. "You wouldn't be a five-star chef. You'd be a *pâtissier*." She said it with a flourish.

Houston's flat expression morphed into a wide grin and he laughed with her. "Where on *Earth* did you hear *that* word?"

Her shoulders lifted and dropped as she picked up her bowl and moved to their little stovetop. There sat a cast iron stove, prepped for the quiche mixture and she was supposed to cook it then cut it into pieces.

Houston still stared at her, a wry smile on his lips. "Just a shrug? That's all I get?"

"I told you, I spent a lot of time learning things when I was younger."

"Yeah. About *flowers*."

Kate turned on the little stove and flashed him a smile. "The things you don't know about me could fill a book."

"Apparently. Would the word *pâtissier* be in that book, too?"

She snickered. "For how much time we spent together as kids, we sure don't know as much as I thought we did."

"Yeah," he murmured. "Strange, isn't it?"

A woman at a nearby table paused and glanced over at him. "Hmm?"

"What?" Houston's brows furrowed.

"You said my name."

Slowly, he shook his head from side to side. "I don't believe so."

The man beside her nudged her with his elbow. "Don't tease the guy." He met Houston's eyes. "Her last name is strange." He held up his hand. "Yes. It's actually strange—and weird."

The woman whacked him with the back of her hand. "You don't get to do that anymore, remember?"

The man chuckled and the two of them got back to their cooking.

Houston's gaze swiveled to Kate. His brows lifted and he pointed his spoon in the couple's direction. "Weird," he mouthed.

Kate leaned in closer to him. "Her name is Avery Strange. She's really nice. Apparently, they have this running joke about her name."

He shook his head but didn't comment. Then, his mouth twitched at the corners, and he chuckled. "You can tell they care about each other, though."

Kate glanced back to where Avery and Logan were murmuring to each other. "Yeah. I noticed that, too." It was a little odd, pretending to be in love while everyone around them was so obviously enamored with one another. Up until this weekend, she hadn't thought much about what her future husband would be like. In fact, she hadn't had much interest in those kinds of things.

Houston's presence beside her confirmed those thoughts had shifted. Feeling his eyes on her, she met his gaze and caught her breath. He studied her with those eyes that could make her melt right into the floor.

Amelia stepped in front of their cooking station, a clipboard in her hand. "Will you two be ready for your interview after the picnic ride?"

Kate stared at her. Right. Amelia was a journalist, and they had to do an interview. That was the whole reason they'd been given this trip free of charge. Her words caught in her throat. She'd felt trapped in a large group of people, but this was just going to be three, four people max. And Houston could answer all the questions. Kate shot a look at Houston.

He nodded. "Absolutely."

Amelia nodded, checked something off on her papers and smiled. "Great. We'll be filming your interview at a location of your choice. Do you have a preference?"

"Filming? I thought this was just for the magazine." Kate's heartrate increased. She hadn't signed up for *that*.

"Yes." Amelia reached over and placed a gentle hand on her arm. "But don't worry. We're only going to pick a few snippets for promotional purposes. We're starting a new magazine and this article will be the jumping-off point. We'll get you together and then we'll do individual ones."

Kate opened her mouth to argue but Houston beat her.

"How about the gardens?" he offered.

Avery nodded. "Perfect. We'll meet there right after the picnic." She wandered off to speak to another couple.

Kate swallowed hard. Her whole body was frozen, stiff and aching. The second Amelia was out of earshot, she whirled around to face Houston. "Did you know they were going to record our interview?" Her voice squeaked. "And that they were going to split us up for questioning?"

He shrugged. "It might have been in the informational packet." His eyes flicked to hers. "Why? You sound worried."

She grabbed his hand and squeezed. "Of course, I sound worried. They're going to ask me some questions about a relationship that *doesn't exist*," she hissed.

Even his charming smile wasn't enough to ease the worry that had begun to constrict her breathing.

"I'm a terrible liar, Houston. You know that."

"It'll be fine. They're probably going to ask how the ranch helped us realize we were meant to be together. I'm sure you could say anything and those jokers would believe it." He nodded to the quiche mixture. "I think your pan is ready."

He started to tug his hand from her grasp then stopped himself. He adjusted it, twisting his grasp around and lifting her fingers to his lips. Tingles started from where he made contact with her and swept through the rest of her body.

"Don't worry. It'll be fine. We've seen enough of this place, you can say whatever you want."

She nodded. "Okay. Yeah, you're probably right."

Houston kissed her once more then dropped her hand and picked up a strawberry. "I'm going to get these started." He smiled again. "Don't worry, Kate. It'll all work out."

THE TRAIL LED them far enough away from the ranch that the hotel was hard to see through the trees. August and Millie took the lead, relaying stories to those who were closer to the front. Kate only caught snippets, but the most interesting thing she heard was that Prince Nicolai had been thrown from a horse out here somewhere and his future wife found him and nursed him to health.

The prince was now king of his country and still managed to visit Silverstone to keep his wife happy. Kate found herself staring at the back of Houston's head. He seemed like the type of guy who would do whatever it took to make *his* wife happy. And she couldn't help but hope that he'd be willing to choose her.

As much as she'd made excuse after excuse against something romantic starting between them, she had to face facts. She was falling for him. With each new private moment that passed between them, she could see it more clearly. She wanted someone sweet. She loved that he baked. There probably wasn't another guy in the universe who could be more kind and caring toward her. No other man she would feel so safe with.

He twisted in his saddle and looked back at her. All it took was a wink and her stomach twisted and flipped. Her heart galloped and the urge to have him wrap his arms around her reared its head. Kate gave him a crooked smile and he faced forward again.

A few minutes later, they arrived at their picnic location. The area had obviously been cleared for prior events. There was a wide hole in the ground where they could set up a bonfire, and surrounding that hole were several fallen logs. The rest of the clearing had been groomed and maintained, the meadow mowed over so the grasses didn't get in the way. Wildflowers dotted the perimeter. Everything about this place just screamed romance.

The leaders of their group came to a stop and turned around to face them.

August waved his hand in the air, quieting anyone who was chatting. "The animals have been trained. They won't leave the area. You're free to let them graze and get a drink from the stream. We invite you enjoy your picnic."

Something touched her knee and she jumped, looking down at Houston. He held both his hands up to her. "You want some help getting down?"

Her face scrunched up and she made a face. "I ride horses for a living. I'm more than capable—"

Houston laughed. "I *know*. I was just asking because I thought—" His eyes grew serious as he studied her. "This whole ride up here, I've been thinking." He rubbed the back of his neck and looked away. A flush crept up his neck as he brought his focus back to her. "Would it be so bad if we tried..." His blush deepened and he cleared his throat. "I sound like a complete idiot. What I wanted to say was that I'm realizing just how much I like you."

"You… *like* me."

His focus swept over the people around them and his voice lowered. "Can we just get our picnic stuff and talk?"

She blinked. "O-okay. Sure." She moved to swing her leg over the saddle, but he was still standing there. He gave her a crooked grin and shrugged as he lifted his hands again.

Kate hoped it looked like she was perfectly fine on the outside, but her heart was thundering faster than it ever had. Inside, she was a complete mess.

She made a show of rolling her eyes but placed her hands on his shoulders anyway and fought to control the flutters going wild in her stomach.

CHAPTER FIFTEEN

HOUSTON COULDN'T TAKE IT BACK NOW. HE'D GIVEN everything away when he'd blurted out that he liked her. What was this? High school? He was a grown adult, fully capable of having a mature conversation. He'd been wrong—about their first kiss and about their relationship not progressing anyway. Admitting that sort of thing was hard, but he'd done it. Losing her because he was too scared to take a chance on exploring these developing feelings was worse than putting himself out there and having her turn him down.

He guided her toward the outskirts of the picnic area by placing his hand on the small of her back. Every time he touched her, the desire to pull her into his arms again grew stronger. But it wasn't just the physical attraction that had changed. He couldn't pinpoint it exactly, but if he had to guess, he would say that the shift had occurred when they were in the gardens. It was in the way her eyes lit up with excitement and joy when she pointed out the flowers.

Little by little, their conversations had uncovered something new that he found he admired.

Who wouldn't be impressed by her ability to wrangle that calf? On top of all that, she'd gotten out of her comfort zone and she was following along with his crazy scheme.

He didn't know one person who would be willing to put up with something like that—at least not for long. Something deep inside made him believe Kate would. She was too good, too patient... too perfect.

"Right here," he murmured as he slowed and pulled a blanket out of his pack.

She turned to face him as he prepared their space. Kate wrapped her arms around herself, her face a mask of unreadability.

What would he do if he found out she didn't have the same inclination to explore whatever was growing between them? Worse—what if she didn't feel it?

Shoving those thoughts down as far as he could, he focused on setting out the food. He wasn't going to find out how she felt until he made her have this conversation. Houston dropped to his knees and set out the containers of food, then looked up at her. She still stood on the edge of the blanket, staring at him.

There was a hint of fear in her eyes—the same look she got when she felt cornered by everyone at the events they'd been to. He couldn't do this when she was looking like she'd bolt at any second.

He rose and held out his hand. Her focus shifted to his offering, then up to his face.

Houston cocked his head. "Come with me."

She slipped her hand into his and he laced his fingers within hers. He tugged on her hand and led her toward the animals that hovered near the stream. They stepped over fallen branches and wove through flowers.

He bent down and plucked a yellow flower. Straightening, he tucked it into her hair above her ear. "It's a stargazer, right?"

Kate's face broke into a smile. "It's a yellow star."

"Right," he chuckled. "You know, it's stuff like that"—he tucked a strand of hair behind her other ear, letting the back of his fingers graze her cheek—"that made me realize I've been blind to you."

"Houston—" Her tone sliced right through him, cutting him to the quick.

He pressed his finger on her lips. "Let me say what I need to say. If I don't, I'm going to chicken out and I never will."

She nodded. "Okay."

"I'm not saying this ranch had anything to do with it. I want to make that perfectly clear. Back home, we don't really spend that much time having conversations like we have. That's when it happened."

"When *what* happened, Houston?"

He took her other hand in his and held both of them. "Something shifted. I care about you." He squeezed his eyes shut. Why was this so hard? "*More*. I care about you more. It's hard to explain, but I don't want us to just be what we've been. Does that make sense?"

Why couldn't he read her like he used to? Had a wall suddenly come up between them?

Her eyes narrowed. "You care about me *more*," she hedged.

"I think I'm in love with you," he blurted.

Kate's eyes widened. "Love."

Houston groaned. "You really know how to make this harder than it has to be, you know that?"

A hint of a smile touched her lips. "Okay. So, to make this clear—you have growing feelings for me." She looked down at their hands clasped together. "What do you want to do about it, Houston?" Her whisper breezed over him, creating goosebumps and chills all at once. "I need you to say it. There can't be any confusion on the matter."

When she lifted her eyes to meet his, the thundering in his chest intensified. "You're so beautiful, Kate."

Her features scrunched into an almost amusing expression.

Houston gave a sharp shake of his head and cleared his throat. "I want to kiss you."

"A kiss." She sounded uncertain, which only made this whole moment all the more unbearable.

"More than a kiss." He cursed under his breath. "I want you, Kate. I want to hold your hand and dance with you. I want to bake macaroons for you and take walks with you. I want to call you mine." His chest heaved as the words escaped his lips.

She chewed on her lower lip, not saying anything. Oh, how much he just wanted to grab her face and capture those lips with his own. If he could show her a window to the feelings that had begun to snowball into something bigger, she'd understand.

But he couldn't do that. Not with Kate. Because if she didn't want him in the same way, he would need to be okay with seeing her around Hickory Hollow as he always had. He tipped his head, probably looking more like a bird than the cowboy he was.

"Well?"

"I can't believe you said all that."

His heart stuttered. "What?"

She blinked a few times, then offered him a shy smile. "Because I want the same things." She shook her head, her eyes darting away and her cheeks blossoming with red. "I can't explain it, but—"

Releasing her hands, Houston placed his on either side of her face and pulled her toward him. His lips brushed hers, happy with stealing just a hint of what they'd experienced before. The fluttering in his chest intensified and his heart began beating like a war drum.

She fit with him. All these years as they matured and became their own people, he hadn't seen it. Maybe he wasn't supposed to. If they had discovered this compatibility when they were younger, there was no telling how it would have ended. How often did high school sweethearts actually make it work? Then, there was the issue of his parents. His mother most definitely would have frowned on such a match. Not because she didn't care for Kate, but because of what could happen if their budding relationship went south. The tension of something like that would most assuredly mess with the flow at the ranch.

The timing had to be perfect, and here it was.

Houston deepened their kiss, slipping one hand behind her head to tilt her face for better access. She wrapped her arms around his neck, locking her fingers together and moving closer to him.

She was everything he wanted and now that he'd found her, he wasn't about to let her slip from his fingers. They'd have to play this carefully. The second they left Silverstone, things would change. They wouldn't be able to hide this from his family.

Houston pulled back and rested his forehead against hers, still breathing heavily. Her lashes lifted and she met his gaze.

"I love you, Houston," she whispered.

A chill ran down his spine. How had he gotten lucky enough to find someone he could be himself with? He'd dated several women in the past and not one of them knew he liked to bake. They all saw what he wanted them to see. And Kate saw it all.

"I love you too, Kate."

Her soft laugh filled him with a happiness he never knew he could experience. "What are we going to tell Georgia?" Her eyes widened and she gasped as she took a step back from him. "What are we going to tell your parents?"

He stepped toward her, enveloping her into a hug. She rested her cheek against his shoulder as they stood like that for a few minutes.

"They'll be happy for us." At least, he hoped so. He'd probably get pulled aside and lectured over the seriousness of what he was doing, but Kate shouldn't have to worry about that.

"Are we crazy?" she murmured. "What if the ranch really is to blame?"

His stomach lurched. "A place can't make people fall in love, Kate. But it gave us the opportunity to spend more time together and discover how right we are for each other."

"I guess you're right." She pulled back, smiling. "But that's not going to stop me from pretending it did—you know, for the interview."

"Whatever makes it easier." Houston chuckled. He leaned forward and kissed her nose. "Maybe we should go eat our food before they start gathering us up to go."

He reached for her hand and they wandered more slowly this time through the wildflowers toward their spot.

Silverstone wasn't special. Magic didn't exist. If it had, their lives would have been very different. They probably would have fallen in love sooner—at Hickory Hollow.

His hand tightened around hers.

Kate glanced at him then placed her other hand over their joined ones. She leaned into him for the rest of their walk back to their blanket.

They settled down next to their meal and he handed her a plate filled with some of the food they'd prepared. Each time he looked up, he caught her staring at him.

"What?" He laughed.

She shrugged. "I just can't believe what's happening."

"I know," he murmured. He took a bite of one of his strawberries. "We should probably discuss a few things before we head home, though."

Kate made a face and he laughed again. He seemed to be laughing a lot with her.

"It's not so bad. You're already basically part of the family. My parents love you, and Georgia is your best friend. The only thing that's going to change is how much time we spend together. The only thing I foresee being a challenge is tearing myself away from you to get my work done."

That blush he adored filled her cheeks and he leaned over their food to press a kiss to her lips. Still close, he whispered, "I don't know what's going to happen, but as long as I have you, I know it's going to be great."

CHAPTER SIXTEEN

KATE MARVELED AT HOW SOMETHING SO SIMPLE AS A SHIFT IN their relationship could make her feel so much joy. All at once, she felt she belonged—more than she ever thought she could. Houston had been right under her nose the entire time.

He popped a piece of the quiche in his mouth and brushed off his hands. "I've been thinking."

Tilting her head, Kate watched as his smile grew and his eyes lit up with excitement.

"What if we switched things up at Hickory Hollow? We've been the place to go to for horse boarding and training, but what if we did something like Silverstone? I'll bet you anything we could compete with them. We could start slow and try to bring people out for the horse riding and dressage camps..." His voice trailed off and he frowned. "What?"

She froze. "Hmm?"

"Why do you look so upset?"

Did she? Right. At some point, she'd started frowning and her brows had lowered. She looked away.

"Tell me what's upsetting you, Kate. I know something is up." Houston edged closer, hooking his finger under her chin and bringing her face up to meet his. "Whatever it is, you can trust me."

Kate's stomach did that little flippy thing again, but this time it wasn't pleasant. It was the kind of feeling she got when she was anxious and didn't want any additional attention brought to her. She withdrew from his touch and shook her head. "It's nothing."

His eyes narrowed and the frown lines in his face deepened. "You can't lie to me, Kate. Even if we weren't taking our relationship to the next level, I'd be able to tell."

She lifted a shoulder. "You know my opinion on making Hickory Hollow something like this place." She gestured around them.

"I thought you liked it here."

"I *do*. But…"

"But?"

A sigh expelled from her chest and she focused on the ground. This was hard to express in a way that didn't make her sound flaky.

"Silverstone has been turned into this getaway. It's more for people who aren't cowboys but want to pretend for a week. It's run by really nice people—but it's not the kind of thing I think would put Hickory Hollow on the map."

Not that she'd want that anyway. "Hickory Hollow is doing great. It provides for your family, your cousins, and it helps keep other ranches afloat. But it's not some vacation spot."

His features had tightened the more she spoke, but he didn't argue with her right away. The warmth from her chest disappeared, leaving her a little chilled despite the summer heat around them.

She worried her lower lip. It was times like these she knew she should have kept her big mouth shut. Houston didn't want to hear this kind of stuff from her. He wanted her to support his dreams. Isn't that what she was supposed to do? That was what this whole partnership was all about. Wouldn't she want the same from him?

Houston rubbed the back of his neck and shifted, putting more space between them. "I don't know if I agree with you." He shot her an almost apologetic look. "Hickory Hollow is my legacy and eventually it will come down to me how to run it. If I fail, then the only one people will blame is—"

"No one would blame you, Houston."

The laugh that slipped from his lips was dry and void of the sweet tone he'd used with her all day. "*Everyone* would blame me. There are jobs and livelihoods at stake here, Kate. I can't just stand back and accept the way things are. The world is in a constant state of change. I have to prepare for that."

For the first time she could remember, it was like she could see the literal weight he carried on his shoulders. She'd never seen him look so anxious over anything. And now he sat here, the worry shrouding him like a storm cloud.

She reached out to him and touched his hand. He looked down at where her fingers rested against his skin, then lifted his gaze to meet hers. Kate offered him a soft smile.

"You still have time to figure it out. And if in the future you want to shift the course of your family's ranch, I won't stand in your way. No one else would have a say in your decision either."

The comfort she'd hoped to bestow on him wasn't reflected in his gaze. He had made it look so easy when he helped her, but this must be a different kind of anxiety. She pressed her lips together tightly, a helplessness overcoming her. How could she expect to help him when she had a hard time getting past her own insecurities?

A small voice whispered it would come in time. They'd just have to stick together and they'd be able to weather the storm. Still, that unease wouldn't let up. A fog of worry draped over her, suffocating that little voice that insisted she not give in to the darkness.

Someone called out for everyone to clean up and the two of them gathered their picnic supplies in silence. Houston was better at grounding her than she was for him—one way they weren't balanced in their relationship. If she'd already discovered one major issue and they hadn't been officially dating for even thirty minutes, how many more would reveal themselves by the time they got home?

Kate shoved that terrible thought aside. She needed to keep a level head. Getting in her own way when it came to something that made her happy would be a sure-fire way for her to end up miserable and alone. And there was no way she'd end up doing that, not when she'd finally found something worth fighting for.

Houston reached for her hand as they wandered through the meadow toward the horses. He squeezed it gently, but it did nothing to settle her stomach. He was so out of her league. She was lucky to find someone interested in her.

He waited for her to get into her saddle before mounting his own steed. The unhappy lines in his face had faded and now he wore a blank stare. Maybe it would continue to morph into the humorous and light expression she'd grown so attracted to, if given enough time.

As they headed down the trail, her thoughts shifted to the impending interview and her insides fluttered. There were several reasons to feel somewhat tense over the whole thing. They had come here under false pretenses, they had only recently discovered their compatibility, and she didn't like being put on the spot.

But with one look in Houston's direction, she knew she could handle it. If he was by her side, holding her hand, she could do anything. He was her anchor.

She only had to figure out how to be the same for him.

Hopefully she'd be able to manage the short amount of time when she'd be doing her part on her own. Of course Houston would be nearby. They wouldn't split them up like *that*.

The ride went faster on their way back than it had been getting to their picnicking location. Everyone in their group left the horses in a corral for the ranch hands to take care of and wandered off in different directions to spend their free time elsewhere.

Kate couldn't find Amelia anywhere nearby. Hadn't she gone with them on the ride?

Houston appeared in front of her, that easy-going smile she loved so much gracing his handsome face. The fog around her heart lifted somewhat and she grinned back.

He wrapped his arms around her, pulling her close. "I guess we should head for the gardens. That's where we're supposed to meet."

Right. She'd nearly forgotten. Houston's warm hands sent shivers through her and she leaned closer to him, yearning for his closeness even more. He captured her mouth in a breath-stealing kiss, causing that fire in the pit of her stomach to ignite. His lips followed her jawline to her ear. Warm breath grazed her earlobe, sending a shock of chills throughout her body.

"I love that I can do this in public," he murmured.

She closed her eyes and swallowed a moan of pleasure. Words couldn't express just how much she agreed with him.

Someone cleared their throat behind him. She jumped and attempted to rip herself from his grasp, but his hands remained securely around her waist as he glanced over his shoulder to the person interrupting their moment.

A blush seared Kate's cheeks when she met Amelia's amused gaze, then shifted her focus to Jake who stood beside her. Jake chuckled and ducked his head closer to Amelia.

"Do you think we should give them some privacy?"

Amelia whacked one of her clipboards into his stomach, eliciting a grunt in response. "Don't tease them. That used to be us." She offered Kate a bright smile. "We were about to take the carriage to the gardens but noticed you guys were still here. We could head over together."

Kate extricated herself from Houston's grip and nodded, ducking her head as she tucked some hair behind her ear. "Sure. Let's do that."

She laced her fingers within Houston's and they followed Amelia and Jake toward the carriage. Houston leaned closer to her, his low voice causing more electrical tension.

"You think they'd notice if we slipped away before we get to the carriage? I bet we could have some fun in that barn."

She sucked in a breath. "*Houston.*" That single word came out in more of a disbelieving laugh than a disapproving statement. "As much as I'd like to avoid this whole interview thing, we can't."

"Darn." He chuckled. "You're probably right. Another time, then."

They didn't sit very close to the other couple on the carriage. In fact, they couldn't have been farther apart. Amelia and Jake murmured to each other, their heads together.

Kate leaned into Houston and rested her head on his shoulder. "Do you think we'll be like that after we've been together that long?"

He trailed the back of his fingers along her bare arm that was closest to his body, raising goosebumps in the wake of his touch. "Nah."

She lifted her head and stared at him, her mouth gaping. "What?"

Houston jutted his chin toward them. "They're probably talking about work. When we cuddle close, we'll be so in love work won't even cross our minds."

Kate blinked, unable to form any words.

A chuckle vibrated from his chest and he draped his arm around her shoulders, pulling her tighter against him. "What?"

"Who knew you were such a romantic?" she murmured.

Cocking his head slightly, he peered down at her. "I suppose I never had any reason to be romantic until I found the person I wanted to be with."

Her features scrunched and he laughed as he pressed a kiss to her furrowed brow.

"What is that look for?" he questioned.

"You're saying you have *never* been able to see yourself with anyone before me? I find that hard to believe."

He shrugged. "I think people can be drawn to others without having that special connection that means more." He touched his chest with his fist. "You can feel it right here, deep down. There's something that sparks to life that is like nothing else."

He gazed at her, his focus unwavering. "I may have dated a good share of women, but none of them have come close to making me feel that. It's how I feel when I'm with you. That's the only way I can describe it."

That unsteady feeling swept through her again. Houston had dated plenty of women over the years. She'd seen them all come and go. And they were all beautiful, confident women who didn't balk at going into a crowded room.

She hadn't dated anyone. Who was to say this infatuation she had for Houston wouldn't fade over time? Kate had nothing to compare it to.

That ugly, sinking feeling only grew stronger the closer they drew to the gardens.

Great. She'd let her insecurities take control. It was like she was standing in front of this amazing guy with her arms empty. What could she even contribute to this relationship? It seemed so one-sided, and she had no idea how to fix it.

CHAPTER SEVENTEEN

HOUSTON COULD HAVE ARGUED. HE'D WANTED TO. KATE WAS wrong when it came to his family's ranch. He could see it —something *would* change around the ranch as he started taking over. No one could stay in the past forever. Complacency bred problems in more ways than one.

But he wasn't about to ruin the start of this relationship. With each passing minute he spent with Kate at his side, his feelings for her deepened. He wanted to shield her from everything out in the world and keep her safe and comfortable. It felt like he was born to do so—a calling of sorts.

He might have already messed with things too much. He'd let his emotions get the better of him, and he'd shown her a less appealing side of him. Kate could read him almost as well as he could read her, maybe even better. If she didn't like what she saw, would she walk away from him?

That would be awkward. What would happen then? They'd see each other on a daily basis and he'd have to relive what it was like to hold her, kiss her, and make her happy. He didn't think he could let another person be that for her.

Honesty. He'd laid it all out on the table when he'd told her how he felt—and maybe he'd been too quick to hand her his heart. She didn't have the experience he did. What if she found someone who could be more for her?

His heart stuttered and grew cold. Houston stifled a shiver. No one knew her like he did and that meant no one could take care of her like he could. Boy, the way he mulled over these thoughts in his head bordered on obsessive. But he wasn't… possessive like that. Was he?

The carriage rolled to a stop, lurching everyone who sat within. The reporters glanced in their direction, offering smiles of encouragement as they stepped from the carriage onto the ground.

Jake gestured toward the gardens. "Our camera guy is all set up near the fountains. Which one of you wants to go first?"

Houston lifted his hand. "I'll do it." He flashed a smile at Kate, who seemed to be melting into his side as they wandered over to the gardens.

Her voice was low enough that Jake and Amelia wouldn't be able to overhear. "I know we're doing this separately, but I'm glad you'll be there so I can look at you whenever I get nervous."

With his arm around her waist, he pulled her tighter against him. "I'll never leave you."

She grinned. "My hero."

They continued following the couple in front of them, an almost comforting silence growing between them. In hindsight, this whole trip was ridiculous. He could admit he'd been rash—jealous, even. Silverstone was a neat place, and it would be an interesting change if they could mimic what the owners had developed here.

His home had so much potential. It just needed to be tapped.

In the clearing, a camera man worked behind a tripod, adjusting something on the recorder. He glanced over his shoulder as they arrived but didn't say anything.

Jake motioned toward the two chairs. "Take a seat, Houston."

Amelia stepped closer to Kate. "You ready to come with me?"

Houston could see the blood draining from Kate's face. He moved between them, a wall of protection. "Where are you going?"

Amelia pointed a pencil toward a trail that led away from the fountain to somewhere behind the hedge. "There will be two parts. One where you're interviewed in front of the camera and one where you just answer a series of questions. We need as much information as we can get to sell this article we're writing."

Houston turned around to face Kate. She looked absolutely sick to her stomach. He faced Amelia once more. "Can't she stay to watch the interview, then we switch?"

Jake shook his head. "There are a few questions we'll ask during the video part where you can't hear each other's answers."

His stomach churned and a rising sense of alarm filled his chest. "Why?"

Jake and Amelia exchanged a smile. "We haven't told anyone, but we thought it would be neat if we layered the clips—kinda like the newlywed game."

But we're not newlyweds. Houston bit down on his tongue and a sharp pain shuddered throughout his body. He shot another look at Kate. Surely, she couldn't have gotten worse.

He was wrong.

Houston shook his head. "Kate doesn't like to be put on the spot like that. I think it would be best—"

"Nonsense." Amelia placed her hand on Kate's back and propelled her toward the path. She looked over her shoulder at them. "Fifteen minutes, Jake."

"I know." He draped his arm around Houston's shoulders. "She keeps me on my toes. That's why I love her."

Houston shrugged out from under Jake's arm. "Kate has anxiety. She needs me to be with her." He attempted to head off toward where the women left but Jake darted in front of him.

"I can't let you do that. It's just a short interview. And Amelia is great at putting her interviewees at ease." He jerked his chin toward the chairs. "Now, let's get our part done so you two can switch. We have another couple coming in thirty minutes."

Shuffling toward the chair, Houston shot one more concerned look to where Kate had disappeared.

"When did you realize you were in love?"

"What?" He glanced at Jake then at the camera. When had they started rolling?

"When did you realize you loved Kate?" Jake flashed him a smile. "I saw the way you were looking at her when she roped that calf. I hear it impressed the rodeo king who lives here, too. Did she do something similar the first time you were here?"

Houston's chest tightened. He swallowed at the hard lump in his throat, but it wouldn't budge. His voice squeaked at first before finally returning to normal as the words tumbled from his lips. "We'd grown up together. I've loved her my whole life."

Jake's brows furrowed and he glanced at the camera, then swung his attention back to Houston. "I guess I need to clarify. At what point while visiting Silverstone Dude Ranch did you realize you wanted to marry her?"

Everything slowed down as his thoughts drifted back to their first day at the ranch together. Kate's unsure features, her pouting lips, the way she smelled. "When I kissed her."

Jake's features broke into a wide smile. "Now we're talking. Tell us more."

Houston stared at his hands resting in his lap, a small smile touching his lips. He lifted his eyes to this stranger. He couldn't believe he was about to tell him the truth about it all. "I was her first kiss."

Jake didn't comment, but his expression said it all. He wanted more.

"And our first kiss—*her* first kiss—took place right here. I wasn't expecting it to affect me so much. I thought kissing her would be like kissing—well, kissing my sister." He shook his head and chuckled. "I should have known better. It was like everything I knew about her was a lie. She was more than I could have ever imagined."

"You knew you were meant to be together based off that one moment."

"Absolutely." Houston stared straight into the camera as if speaking directly to Kate. "I don't care how difficult things become. I know in my heart that we were meant for each other. You were destined to be mine, and I will spend every day proving that to you."

Jake shifted in his seat, adjusted the clipboard in his hands, and asked his next question. It grew increasingly hard to focus on each one as Jake listed them off like they were nothing. The questions only solidified what he knew to be true. This wasn't some superficial infatuation he had for Kate. Questions about silly things like favorite color or favorite foods paled in comparison. Jake asked him what he admired about Kate. Where he saw them five or ten years from now.

COWBOY'S DESTINY

Of course, he was already supposed to be married to her, so Houston couldn't exactly mention that. But the thought of actually proposing made his insides grow weak. It was pleasant and terrifying all at once—and exactly what he wanted for his future.

Finally, Kate wandered back into the clearing, appearing more at ease. She spoke quietly to Amelia but then her focus shifted and their eyes locked. Yes. He couldn't think of anything more that he would want other than to have her to call his own for the rest of his life. He wanted to be her everything.

"What is it about Kate that you can't live without?" Jake wrapped up with the last question and Houston answered without thinking.

"Her smile."

As if she'd heard his answer from where she stood, she flashed him a grin that made his insides boil. One day, he was going to make her his wife. There wasn't a doubt in his mind. It had taken him all of one day to realize something he should have figured out years ago. He'd been so blind. So much time wasted.

"Kate, your turn." Jake waved his arm in an arc through the air.

Houston moved toward her and they paused in the middle. He snickered. "Do you feel like we're hostages being traded?"

She snorted, a dimple forming in her left cheek.

He brushed the back of his knuckles along her jaw. "Never stop doing that."

"Doing what?" Kate peered up at him, her guileless eyes large.

"Smiling."

Her cheeks colored.

"Come on, love birds. We have another interview right after you." Though Jake's voice sounded bored, the undertone was teasing.

Kate glanced at Jake and back to Houston. "I should probably—"

He nodded. "Love you."

"I love you, too," she whispered.

"I'll never get tired of hearing you say that."

CHAPTER EIGHTEEN

KATE SETTLED ONTO THE CHAIR BESIDE JAKE, SWALLOWING down the anxiety that seemed to never leave. She'd be happy when she could get back to Hickory Hollow and be done with this charade. Yes, she was now dating Houston. But that didn't change the fact that they'd lied to get here.

Amelia had been shrewd with her questions—kind, but shrewd. At any given second, Kate expected her to jump out of her seat and point an accusing finger, yelling, "Liar!"

Now, as Kate sat beside Jake, the modicum of peace she'd enjoyed while speaking with Amelia had dissipated. The camera seemed like this big black hole in her peripheral. At any moment, she'd be sucked into its abyss due to her duplicity.

"Relax. Amelia's questions are harder than mine." Jake leaned forward, holding his hand to the side of his mouth, "But you didn't hear it from me." He settled back in his chair and grinned. "My questions are mostly the emotional stuff."

Great. This was where she'd have the hardest time lying. With Amelia, it was mostly fact-based. How long had they known each other before getting together, was she expecting to fall in love with him, et cetera.

Kate squirmed, clasping and unclasping her hands. She shook them out a few times and attempted to push through all the tells she knew she had.

"When did you realize you loved Houston?"

She glanced down at her lap and a smile tugged at her lips before she lifted her face once more. "When he let me wrangle that calf."

Jake's brows shot up. He cleared his throat and adjusted in his seat. He looked to the camera and drew a finger across his throat.

Kate paled. "Wait, I didn't mean that—"

Jake scooted across his chair until he was close enough to speak in a whisper. At least he didn't look mad. "Kate, how long have you and Houston been together?"

Her face flamed red.

He tilted his head slightly, eyeing her like a hawk might a small mouse.

Kate's mouth went dry, a stark contrast to her damp palms. She wrung her hands together and looked away. "Just a few months."

"*Kate*."

She shot out of her seat. "I knew this was a bad idea. From the second he told me to come, I *knew* something would go wrong. I should have never listened to him—"

Suddenly, Jake was in front of her, his hands gently grabbing onto hers. His eyes were narrowed, but not dangerous. "Answer the question."

Tugging her hands from his grasp, she took a step back. "Does it matter? You know we lied."

"It does."

Kate threw her hands into the air and looked anywhere but at the man interviewing her. "Today!"

She didn't think his face was capable of showing more shock, but boy, was she wrong. She groaned and raked her hands through her short hair. "I can't believe I blew it."

"Take a seat, Kate. I'm still going to interview you."

She froze, rooted to her spot. Nothing was capable of making her move. *"What?* You're joking. Tell me you're joking."

His mouth quirked into a smile and he studied her. Something in his gaze seemed to make everything stand still. Her legs didn't feel like her own as she moved the few feet back to her chair and lowered herself into it. She kept her eyes trained on him, her body stiff as a board.

Looking down at his clipboard, Jake pulled a pen out of his pocket and tapped it against his chin. His eyes flicked to meet hers. "You've been together since this afternoon. Officially."

Numbly, she nodded.

"How long have you two known each other?"

She swallowed and her face flushed. "I was orphaned, and my uncle worked on his ranch. When my last remaining relative died, his family sort of took me in. We were practically raised together."

Jake's chin lifted as he appraised her. "Interesting. And you knew you were in love only this morning?"

Kate crumpled, her hands covering her face. "Are we going to get in trouble?"

"On the contrary."

She peeked through her fingers.

He chuckled. "Kate, you and Houston are a prime example of what can happen at this ranch—and it's occurring in real time. I feel like I *should* be asking you why you two came up here for a couples retreat. But Amelia and I agreed to stick with the preapproved questions."

Never had she seen such pure and unadulterated curiosity in someone's face. Jake tapped his pen against his chin once more as if thoughtfully considering the consequences of going rogue. The cogs whirred and he fidgeted. Finally, he heaved a sigh.

"You're not going to tell anyone, are you?" she whispered.

Jake shook his head. "There's no real point. The article is about people who found love at Silverstone Ranch, not those who managed to get through our vetting process and attend the retreat for their own personal reasons. Besides, it's clear you two are in love." He flashed her a smile. "Anyone with eyes can see that."

Kate's spine went limp and she slouched into her chair. "I'm so sorr—"

He held up a hand. "Don't worry about it. I'm going to get the camera rolling again, and I just want you to answer honestly. Can you do that?"

"But wouldn't that ruin your little game thing you're doing?"

Jake lifted a shoulder. "Just humor me. If we can't use your footage, I'm sure we have plenty that will work."

His steady gaze, something that would have put her on edge before, seemed to have the opposite effect. Kate nodded.

"Okay."

Jake motioned to the camera guy and then faced her. "Tell me about when you knew you loved Houston."

She glanced at the camera and then back to Jake. "Houston and I grew up on a ranch."

Another brow lift from Jake. Kate offered a shy smile and touched her hair again.

"He's usually really competitive. And he's good at what he does. But there are some areas where I excel."

Jake pointed his pen toward her. "Like wrangling calves."

Kate nodded. "Right. So, when that competition came up, I mentioned that I could put all the contestants to shame. And he agreed. None of the women were being asked to participate, but when August came by to offer the rope to

Houston…" She shrugged. "That was the moment I knew he cared about me."

"And you cared about him."

"Right. I mean, what kind of guy would step aside when he could show off his skills? It was obvious everyone who was lassoing that calf had virtually no experience. Houston could have smoked them."

"But not like you."

She let out a soft laugh. "I guess I sound a little too sure of myself."

"I wouldn't say so." Jake lifted his ankle and rested it on his knee. "I heard Tyson Lee spoke to you personally about joining his crew."

And just like that, all the worry and fretting left her. Kate beamed at him. "He mentioned I have a natural talent and I could do very well in the rodeo."

Jake smiled back. "Houston mentioned that particular talent was something he admired."

Kate blinked. "He did?"

He flipped through the pages on his clipboard. "Sorry?"

She shook her head. "Nothing."

Jake met her gaze. "What would you say you admire most about Houston?"

Without missing a beat, she straightened in her seat, then leaned forward so she could emphasize each word. "His calming presence. It doesn't matter how bad my state of mind is, Houston can bring me off a ledge with one look, one touch." Her face flushed.

That was probably too personal. She shouldn't be sharing their more intimate moments. Kate looked away once more, fighting the embarrassed smile that threatened to burst from within her.

Jake asked her a series of other questions, most of them easy to answer. If she had been just a little more cautious in the beginning, she might have gotten through the interview without spilling their secret.

Hopefully Houston wouldn't mind when she inevitably told him.

The last question Jake asked threw her off guard. "Where do you see yourself in ten years?"

A chill swept down her spine and she let out a laugh that sounded more like she was choking. "Well, of course, with everything being so new and fresh, I'd love to say that we'd be married with a few kids." She looked away. "But you can never guarantee something like that. It's hard to say where we would be. All I know is that I want to enjoy the time I have with him now. Honestly, I'd be happy if time stopped right now in this moment and I could revel in the happiness I've found with him."

When she looked up, she half-expected Jake to be rolling his eyes.

It was odd that he'd taken the more emotional questions. In general, guys didn't have the disposition for stuff like this. But Jake seemed different. Was he actually enjoying this? The small smile he wore appeared to answer her question.

He slapped his hands on his legs and rose to his feet. "Thank you for answering my questions, Kate."

She glanced toward where Houston would soon be returning, then she stood. "I really am sorry about all this."

"Don't give it a second thought," Jake assured her. "This is the place where I fell in love with Amelia. Actually, that isn't true; I'd fallen for her before I came here. We had a history, too." He winked. "We were just really good friends. But when we came here, it gave me the opportunity to convince her that I meant more to her than she had accepted for herself."

He glanced around the gardens then swung his focus back to Kate. "There sure is something special about this place. It might not be magic, but it gives people who visit the chance to have an open mind when it comes to love."

"That's what I keep saying."

Kate jumped as Houston came up beside her, slipping his arm around her waist and brushing a tender kiss to her cheek. She leaned into him, noting the pointed look Jake was giving her.

"You two make a handsome couple. I'm happy for you both." He moved away from them toward the cameraman.

Houston shot Kate a funny look. "What was *that* all about?"

She grimaced. "I have to tell you something."

His brows furrowed and his whole body stiffened. "Uh oh."

If she could tell him it wasn't bad, she would. She just wasn't sure. Kate grasped his hand and tugged him down a different path. "I don't want you to be mad."

"That's not making me feel any better," he muttered as she all but dragged him around a corner and put as much distance as she could between them and their interviewers.

Finally, she stopped, releasing his hand and fixing her eyes on him. "Jake knows."

"Jake knows *what*?" he drawled.

Kate moistened her lips and leaned toward him. "He knows we're not married."

He stilled for just a second before his head whipped around to look in the direction they'd come from. "*What*?" he hissed.

She flinched. "It's okay. He said he wasn't interested."

Houston grasped her upper arms within his hands. "I don't believe that for a moment."

"Okay. He *was* interested, but he wasn't going to—"

"What did you tell him?"

"Nothing." Kate swallowed, her eyes searching his. "Nothing," she repeated.

He released her and ran both hands into his hair. Pacing in front of her, his concern tumbled from his mouth in a string of questions. "How did he find out? Did he say we'd be penalized for lying about why we are here? Is he going to tell anyone?"

Kate stepped in front of him, cutting him off. "He's not going to tell anyone because he said we're obviously in love so we're not breaking any rules."

At least, that was the gist of it. She cleared her throat and continued.

"If he's not going to tell anyone, then I don't think we'll be charged anything or even kicked out. And it's my fault he found out." She grabbed both of his hands in hers and traced her thumbs over his knuckles. "I told him when I knew I was in love with you, and I was so caught up in the moment I didn't even realize what I'd said until it was too late."

Everything seemed to slow down. Houston acted as if he had forgotten the dilemma they were currently stuck in. The corners of his mouth twitched and lifted into an almost silly grin.

"What did you tell him?"

She shifted her weight from one foot to the other. "When you let me wrangle that calf."

"Really?"

Kate nodded. "It was more than keeping me calm. You wanted to help me be in my element. You didn't jump in to show off—you let me shine. There aren't many men out there who would do the same."

He tugged on her hands, pulling her against him. A soft grunt escaped her lips and she wrapped her arms around his neck. "I like seeing you happy," he murmured.

"So, you're not mad?"

Houston frowned momentarily. "It's not ideal... What *did* he say about wanting to know why we were here?"

"Just that he was curious."

"And you didn't tell him?"

She shook her head. "I don't think it really matters anymore. Right? The reasons we're here have shifted."

"Yeah." He leaned down and rubbed the tip of his nose against hers. "You could definitely say that."

CHAPTER NINETEEN

HOUSTON STOOD IN THE GARDENS WITH THE OTHER MEN WHO were attending the couples' retreat. Most of them chatted amongst themselves, apparently having made a few friends. But he'd grown more on edge by the hour.

Jake could have been lying to Kate to keep her at ease. It was clear to everyone out here that she needed help to stay grounded. One wrong turn and she could hyperventilate or have a panic attack.

He paced back and forth near the entrance to the gardens, attempting to do so leisurely so it didn't look like he was stressing too much.

There had been fine print when sending in the request to be included in this retreat. *Stupid*. He should have read through it all. What if there were financial repercussions, or worse? He was surprised Jake hadn't come talk to him privately.

It shouldn't matter, right? Kate was correct. His reasons for being here had shifted from proving the ranch *wasn't* magic to really getting a feel for how Silverstone was being run. He still wasn't convinced that Hickory Hollow couldn't be improved upon. A small part of him wanted to believe that Silverstone held the key to that enhancement.

A heavy hand landed on his shoulder and he held in a yelp as he jumped. Houston turned around to find Lucas smiling broadly.

"You should take it easy or you'll wear a hole in the ground."

Houston glanced down at the concrete pavers and shot Lucas a disbelieving look.

Lucas laughed. "Joking." He jutted his chin toward the entrance of the gardens. "Nervous?"

Letting out a strained laugh, he shrugged out from Lucas's touch. "How can you tell?"

The man folded his arms and grinned at Houston. "You look like I did when I got left at the altar, and we both know how that turned out. You'll be fine."

Houston scoffed. "You have no idea *why* I'm nervous."

"If I were a betting man…" Lucas shook his head. "You'd be surprised at how observant some of the people here can be."

His whole body stiffened. They'd been careful. Everything was unraveling. How had this guy found out about his secret?

Lucas lifted a shoulder. "Whatever is going on between the two of you, it'll all work out." He flashed Houston one more smile. "If I can be left at the altar and end up happy after all is said and done, I'm certain you and Kate will be okay."

Houston's brows furrowed. "What are you implying?"

"Only that relationships aren't easy. Sometimes, you'll run into a roadblock you didn't see coming. In a few months, none of it will matter."

"You think we're... having a fight?" Relief eased the tightness in his chest.

Lucas held up both hands. "I'm only saying that I've noticed the two of you have a different kind of dynamic. And I wanted to let you know that nothing is so hard that you can't get through it if you work together." He shoved his hands in his pockets and offered one more smile. "Just remember that."

Houston watched him walk away, more confused than he'd like to admit. He didn't think he had acted any differently toward Kate than the other people here treated their partners. But maybe Lucas had seen something Houston hadn't realized. Was Houston closing himself off from Kate in some way?

His thoughts were disrupted when, collectively, the men seemed to turn toward the entrance of the gardens.

The women wandered in, each one clad in a pair of fitted jeans, boots, a white blouse, and white cowboy hat. Their hair and make-up seemed to have been done up for just this event.

Houston's focus homed in on Kate immediately. He'd seen her in such outfits before, granted they were more worn down.

The men around him whistled and bellowed catcalls. Houston strode toward Kate, drinking in every last detail. "Wow," he murmured. "You can sure pull off that look."

She rolled her eyes and pushed his shoulder with her fingertips. "I wear this stuff all the time." She motioned to the other women and leaned in close to him, almost conspiratorially. "I think this whole charade was to trigger some kind of emotion from when they fell in love."

He barely registered her words, unable to drag his eyes from her face. She had opted for minimal make-up. Her lashes were curled and her cheeks held the barest hint of color.

Kate's features scrunched and she tilted her head. "You okay?"

"Yeah. Of course. You just—" He let out a low whistle. "You just look amazing."

Her expression smoothed and she smiled. "Thank you. You're not half-bad yourself."

He glanced down at the clothes he'd picked out. They hadn't been told to dress in any particular way, so he'd just donned his usual jeans and white T-shirt. "It's nothing compared to your get-up."

She shoved him again, but a soft laugh escaped her lips. The sound wrapped around him like a warm hug.

Houston draped his arm around her shoulder and pulled her close. "Do you know why they wanted to do dinner out here?"

"Because it's beautiful?" She laughed again.

"Oh, I thought there might be some significance to this place."

She reached over and placed a hand against his chest as they followed the group heading farther into the gardens. "I think it's just because this place is the most romantic part of the whole ranch." Kate rested her head on his shoulder, snuggling closer to him.

He reached up and took the hat from her head with one hand, then turned his head and pressed a kiss to her hair. "I'm so lucky you're mine," he murmured.

Kate let out a hum of agreement.

They continued walking along paths he hadn't explored before. The lights from all the buildings faded away as they turned and wove down the path. The shrubbery grew taller and it almost felt like they were being swallowed by it all. Then, they arrived in another clearing that had been set up with tables and chairs.

Candles and floral centerpieces sat on fine linen tablecloths. Each place setting was designed for one of those fancy five-course meals.

He exchanged an impressed look with Kate, and they picked their table on the outskirts of the group. Once everyone was seated, Benjamin Greene seemed to materialize out of nowhere. He offered the group a wide smile.

"This place holds a special part in my heart. My daughters were raised here, and I got to spend the best days of my life here with my true love." His voice broke. "I know she would have loved what this place has become and what it represents. In a world that values the opinions of strangers on the internet or watching the next viral video, we have created an escape. Silverstone Dude Ranch will always be here for those who are a little lost—for those who need to find something." His gaze trailed over everyone seated. "For each of you, that was love. For others, it might be confidence or joy."

Chills ran up and down Houston's arms, lifting goose-bumps he couldn't shake.

"I joke that this wonderful spot is a place to find love, but that's only because I miss my sweet Iris. I want everyone to find what I had—what each of you has. I hope you will cherish the memories and relationships you have made while visiting Silverstone Ranch. And come again any time you'd like."

Applause and cheers filled the air. Kate laughed, glancing at Houston again before bringing her attention to the next speaker.

Houston observed as couples held hands, smiled at each other, or leaned over their tables to kiss. None of these people were fakes. They'd all found the missing piece of their lives here at this ranch. Ben had made something amazing happen, and probably without even trying.

He brought his gaze back to the woman in front of him. He'd found something he didn't even realize he needed. He had more purpose somehow—and she could become the partner he'd need to make Hickory Hollow thrive.

Another cheer went up and a few waiters wandered through the clearing, carrying platters covered by silver covers. His stomach twisted pleasantly as he let all these realizations wash over him. He could do anything with

Kate by his side. She was the perfect combination of strong and soft that he was drawn to. Who else could hold her own in front of a beast, and yet make him feel like she still needed him to rescue her?

Houston reached across the table and grabbed her hand in his. He turned it over and traced her palm with his finger. "We go home tomorrow."

She nodded, gaze trained on what he was doing.

"I want you to know something." He couldn't believe he was even thinking it, but he already knew. Deep down, he knew he wanted her to be by his side for the rest of their lives. Nothing else would do.

Kate lifted her face to meet his gaze, her wide, chocolate eyes the epitome of innocence and at the same time, fire.

"Kate, I want to—"

A waiter placed a tray before them and took off the lid with a flourish. "Smoked trout blinis with crème fraîche and dill."

Her eyes dropped to the hors d'oeuvres then bounced to meet his. "This looks amazing."

The waiter gestured toward the food. "The smoked trout atop these small pancakes holds a surprising cayenne pepper kick. It is finished off by a dollop of crème fraîche and a hint of anise dill to balance the fish's smokey flavor." He bowed and strode away.

Kate's smile spread over her whole face. "I've never had trout before. Do you think Wesley made these?"

Houston swallowed back his confession, the mood lost from when he'd received his revelation. He'd tell her he had every intention of marrying her when they had another charged moment, and she could see the intensity of what he felt for her.

He offered her an encouraging smile. "I'm sure he did. This looks exactly like what a five-star chef would make to show off."

Kate gave him a warning look. "Be nice."

"What? It does." He chuckled and reached for the food.

She took a bite and flinched, her hand coming beneath her chin as if she'd missed something. Boy, he could stare at her all day. What a difference a few days had made in their lives.

He'd never regret coming out to this ranch, ever.

CHAPTER TWENTY

EACH COURSE THAT WAS BROUGHT OUT TO THEM WAS BETTER than the last. Kate had never tasted food this fancy in her whole life. Yes, she'd spent all that time on a ranch in Texas with no money for travel—or to experience anything new and exciting. But the Shipleys were wealthy. They had access to the finer things. They'd gone on trips as a family, but of course they didn't take the little girl who lived with the grumpy old wranglers.

A rock settled into the pit of her stomach. She never blamed them. She couldn't have asked for anything more than they'd already agreed to. Heck, they'd even made sure her uncle could clothe her and get her an education. And they'd given her a job and a roof over her head long after Ted had passed.

Things were about to change between herself and Houston, but somehow, it didn't feel like they'd change that much. She might spend more time with them, but Houston wasn't really the traveling type. What if she wanted to see the world before she settled down?

She peeked at him from beneath her lashes as they enjoyed the crème brûlée that had been served a few moments ago. Loving Houston was easy—too easy. She could see herself following him like a puppy wherever he went. He could make her feel more secure and loved than anyone she'd ever met.

And yet it felt like something was missing.

Ben's words filled her mind. Maybe the thing she was finding at this ranch wasn't supposed to be love, after all. What if she'd come here to realize she needed more in her life—more before she settled down? What if Tyson Lee had been the trigger for her to carve her own path?

Chest growing tight, Kate put her fork down and stared at her food, no longer hungry. If she didn't build up the courage to try something new, would she ever do it? If Houston was always protecting her from what scared her the most, would she ever grow into her greatest potential?

"You okay?"

She shot a look in his direction, forcing a smile and nodding. She'd tell him in the morning. Kate refused to ruin an evening like this because of the turmoil swirling in her stomach.

Houston wiped his mouth then cocked his head slightly. "*Kate*." She could almost hear the warning in the way he emphasized her name.

As if against her will, she flinched.

"I can tell something's bothering you. Is it the food?"

She shook her head. "The food is wonderful."

He glanced around the area where everyone sat, eating and murmuring to each other. "Are you feeling a little crowded?"

Kate straightened in her seat. "Actually, no."

That was strange. She'd never been in a large group setting without getting twinges of that anxiety she was so familiar with. Now, she sat in front of Houston, surrounded by several strangers, and she hadn't given them a single thought.

"Then what is it?" Houston reached for her hand and brought it to his lips. His touch elicited a charge of electricity that rippled through her body and started her heart pumping.

Would it be so bad to accept the path she was currently taking? Houston was a good man with a lot to offer. This could be a case of just wanting something she didn't have. There were no guarantees that she would end up being a rodeo star, anyway. Just because she had good instincts didn't mean it would correlate to her being successful.

He squeezed her hand, dragging her back to the present. "Kate," he whispered, "you can tell me. Anything. I want you to know that."

She nodded, swallowing down the bitterness that seemed to threaten the happiness she'd felt when she'd arrived in the gardens. Her eyes dropped to the dessert. "I think I want to take some time off from Hickory Hollow and join Tyson Lee on his rodeo tour."

An unsettling quiet dropped around her. Somewhere in the back of her mind, she could tell that it wasn't affecting the other guests. It was just her.

Everything seemed to slow down as Houston pulled his hand away.

She looked up at him, finding his features a tight mask of unreadability. His jaw was set in a hard angle, his mouth pressed into a firm line. Even his eyes seemed vacant of the warmth she was so used to seeing.

"I thought we'd talked about that already."

Her mouth dropped open. "What?"

Houston grabbed his fork again and fiddled with it, his focus shifting to his plate. "Yeah. Tyson said he wanted to invite you to the rodeo thing, and you said no."

"No. *You* said no." She clasped her hands in her lap so tight her fingers turned white. "Then I got mad at you because you were making decisions without talking to me."

"And you agreed that it probably wouldn't work out."

She bristled. "I didn't *agree* to anything."

She racked her brain for that conversation. The whole thing was muddled. It was possible she'd admitted he had a point. Since then, her confidence had changed, grown into something she was just beginning to understand.

Kate scowled at him. "I thought relationships were supposed to be about give and take."

He matched her glare with one of his own and his voice lowered. "And all you want to do is take."

Her mouth dropped open. "How in the world are you coming to that conclusion? My decision to change my career path has nothing to do with *taking* something from you."

Houston clamped down his mouth and shook his head. "Forget it. You wouldn't understand."

"Try me," she bit out through gritted teeth.

"What?"

"Please explain how my interest in something hurts you. Because from my point of view, it looks like you just want to *control* me."

Houston shot out of his seat, drawing curious glances. He kept his voice low, but his body language was clear to anyone watching. They were having a fight.

"Control? Is that what you think I'm doing?" He shook his head. "You *need* me. We both know it. You're so lost without an anchor—and *I* provide that for you."

He closed his eyes briefly, taking in a deep breath and letting it out. "Let's not fight about this now. We go home tomorrow and we can talk about it then."

"No."

His eyes shot open and he stared at her like she'd slapped him across the face.

Slowly, she rose to her feet. "First of all, you're wrong. I've been doing fine my entire life without you there to shield me from the little things I struggle with. And frankly, I'm beginning to wonder if it's a good thing. You won't be able to help me forever, Houston. What if you didn't want to be with me anymore but you made me dependent on you? Do you have any idea what that would do to me?" She shook her head. "I need to know I can trust you to help when things become too much, but I also need to make sure you know when to step back and let me fly. I'm not your little project."

Kate threw down her napkin. "I'm going to talk to Tyson about the rodeo and you can't stop me." She stormed through the area, past the waiters and disappeared behind a wall of vines.

~

HIS HEART PLUMMETED, going down, down, down as it charged toward a cavernous pit in his stomach. What had just happened?

Everything around him faded into an inky blackness that he couldn't see through. All he could feel was the pounding of his erratic heartbeat. His blood rushed in his ears, and he couldn't breathe.

Kate wanted to leave him. She wanted to run off and become some fancy rodeo star. Was he not enough for her? Why would she want to escape from the life they could have at Hickory Hollow? Their ranch might not be like Silverstone, but it was home. It was perfect.

Perfect.

For all his insistence at changing the place he called home, he couldn't think of one thing that was more important than stopping Kate from making this mistake. She might not realize it, but she needed him just as much as he needed her. If she left, she might break.

Houston moved to stand just as someone settled into Kate's chair. His head snapped up and he came face to face with Jake.

Great. This was the last thing he wanted to deal with at the moment.

"Not now, Jake."

The columnist folded his arms and seemed to settle even deeper into the chair he sat down in. "That's not very friendly. I thought we had a good time this afternoon."

Houston stifled a groan. With each passing second, Kate was getting farther from him. He needed to stop her from finding Tyson and making a terrible mistake. "It's not you. It's—"

Jake chuckled. "*You*? Sorry, but I'm already in a relationship."

Houston's shocked reaction must have been hilarious because Jake laughed.

"*Kidding*. I'm guessing this has something to do with Kate storming off."

"It's none of your business," Houston snapped.

Jake didn't even flinch. His clear eyes and blank features were the perfect combination to give Houston pause.

"What do you want?"

"I thought I might be able to help."

A bark of laughter escaped Houston's throat. "You're kidding."

Jake shook his head. "I'm actually pretty good with relationship stuff—well, except for my own. But Amelia can be something else." He leaned forward and whispered, "Don't tell her I said that."

"No offense, but you don't know anything about me or Kate."

Jake arched a brow. "You think so?"

"I know so."

The man in front of him seemed to be studying his nails as he contemplated his words. "I'm sure Kate told you that I'm aware you aren't supposed to be here."

Houston stiffened. "She also said you told her you wouldn't do anything about it."

Jake lifted a shoulder. "I won't. But don't you think I might have some insight into what makes the two of you tick? I did interview you."

"We could have easily lied."

Jake appraised him. "True. But you and I both know that Kate is a terrible liar. Aren't you the least bit curious how she answered her questions?"

Houston fidgeted in his seat. She'd told him a few of the things she'd said, but not everything. There were some pretty personal questions they'd gone over.

He shook his head vehemently. "It doesn't matter how she answered them. I know the important parts. Like the fact she wouldn't be able to survive out in the real world without me to be there for her."

Jake laughed.

Fury erupted in Houston's stomach. "What?"

"That's a little harsh, don't you think?"

"What do you mean?"

Jake leaned forward and jabbed his finger on the table. "Did you not hear one thing that Mr. Greene said in his speech?"

Houston frowned. "He said this place isn't magic even though he wants it to be."

Jake threw his hands in the air. "It's men like you that give us a bad rap. Read between the lines. No, just go over what he said in its entirety. He said this place is where people discover what's missing from their lives. Yes, love is a big part of it, which is why *that* is the focus of our article. But it's not always the case. For *you*, it was love."

Houston looked away, the scowl still on his face.

"But for Kate, it wasn't."

His hands tightened into fists at his sides. Maybe he needed to pray for the strength not to clock this guy for all his bad assumptions. "Yeah? Well, what do you think it was for her?"

Jake went quiet, forcing Houston to meet his eyes again. The man folded his arms once more and offered a smile.

"If I weren't such a good guy, I would make you figure it out on your own."

Houston huffed. "That doesn't make sense."

He ignored Houston and continued. "But you're obviously so self-centered and blind you can't see how much she's changed. I don't know if you paid any attention, but there have been cameras rolling at every event, just to get footage—not picking up anything in particular. Would you like to see the day you two arrived? Heck, I'll show you everything. You'll see. With each clip, she changes. It's like she came here as a caterpillar and she's going to leave as a butterfly."

"Stupid analogy," Houston muttered.

Jake laughed again. "Yeah, probably. But it's true. Come on. I'll show you what I'm talking about."

CHAPTER TWENTY-ONE

KATE MADE IT NEARLY TO THE BARN BEFORE HER STEPS slowed. She wouldn't have been surprised if steam rose from her body due to the fury she was currently dealing with.

What right did Houston have to tell her what to do? None. *That's right, none*, she admonished. Theirs was a new relationship—and one, admittedly, that excited her. However, the rodeo opportunity Tyson had offered was a once-in-a-lifetime chance for her to find herself.

Her legs trembled and her whole body felt numb. How was she supposed to choose which path to take? Why couldn't Houston be the kind of guy she'd read about in books? Wasn't her true love supposed to be there for her every step of the way, even if it scared him? She needed his support, not an argument.

The evening had grown cooler and goosebumps rose on her arms, though due to the air or the route her thoughts had taken, she couldn't be sure. Kate stepped inside the barn and pulled up against the wall, her fingers tracing the texture of the wood grain behind her. She lifted her chin and inhaled a deep, shuddering breath, fighting the hot, stinging tears that built up behind her eyes.

After her parents' deaths, she'd felt like an afterthought. From being raised by an elderly great uncle to helping out at Houston's ranch, she had never felt like she was wanted. Appreciated, yes, but never *wanted*.

Now, someone wanted her, and not just because they needed a warm body to fill a position. Tyson wanted her because she had a natural talent and a skill that was valued.

Why couldn't Houston see how special that was?

She hadn't wanted to break up. That wasn't the point of leading their conversation down that path. What she really wanted was for Houston to show even a degree of pride or excitement for her and to tell her he'd be waiting when she was done.

That was how someone in love would have acted.

Right?

A sigh escaped Kate's chest and she slid down the wall, sitting in a ball on the floor. She needed to stop dwelling on this. Her decision had been made. It wasn't forever, and she didn't doubt that Dakota and Brady would accept her back to work at Hickory Hollow again.

The only thing she'd be losing was her relationship with Houston.

The ache in her chest intensified. She'd never felt so loved by someone. And she'd thrown that away because she wanted to follow her heart.

"Is this seat taken?"

Kate jumped and peered through the darkness at a figure standing over her. "Avery?"

She moved to sit beside Kate. "I figured you could use a friend. Based on the streaks left on your cheeks, I'd say I was right."

Kate's eyes widened. She hadn't realized the tears had actually slipped down her face. Wiping at them with the back of her hand, she let out a strangled laugh. "I'm fine, really. Just having a bad day is all."

She stared straight ahead. If she looked Avery in the eye, the emotion she fought so hard to keep locked up would be released again.

Avery leaned her head against the wall with a *thunk*. "Everyone tells you falling in love is supposed to be easy. But they never tell you how hard it is to stay in love."

She turned slightly, her focus on Kate.

Shifting, Kate avoided meeting Avery's eyes despite the feeling that the woman was drilling her focus into her.

"You want to talk about anything?"

Kate's eyes flicked to Avery and back to the darkness of the barn. "Not really."

Avery was nice and all, one of Kate's favorite people in this group. But she was still a virtual stranger. Spilling the reasons why Kate had just had a fight with her fake husband was the last thing she wanted to do with someone she barely knew.

Avery shrugged. "I told Logan not to wait up for me."

Whipping her face around to look at Avery, Kate gaped at her. "Tonight is the special night. Isn't he going to be mad that you left him?"

Despite the shadows, Kate could see the soft smile on Avery's lips. "Logan understands when I have something I need to do. Tonight will be special, but we were here a few months ago. I'd say helping out a friend who needs it is more important."

She reached over and placed a hand on Kate's knee. "Not that tonight isn't important. But I have the rest of my life to spend with him, and tomorrow you and I will part ways."

Kate's brows furrowed. "But you don't know me."

"I know that I like you. I know that you're hurting. And I know that I might be able to help." Avery settled back against the wall. "I can wait until you're ready to find the words to let it out. I'm patient."

As much as she would like to bounce ideas off Avery, Kate knew she couldn't. They couldn't risk another person finding out that they'd lied about why they were there. And Kate couldn't tell Avery what was really bothering her without starting at the beginning.

Kate stifled a groan. There was no one else she could talk to. The Shipleys didn't know about her relationship with Houston. Georgia was the closest thing she had to a friend, and she would be more interested in discussing her relationship rather than her dilemma about joining the rodeo.

What was she supposed to tell Avery? That even though she was married, her 'husband' didn't want her to leave him to go on an adventure? Of course he wouldn't. Kate would be the villain in this scenario.

She closed her eyes. "Thanks for the offer, but I don't think there's anything you can do. It's complicated."

"You'd be surprised at just how simple things become when you say them out loud."

Kate shook her head. "You don't understand. I can't give you the whole story. So your opinion or advice would be skewed."

"Try me." Avery tilted her head and offered an encouraging smile. "Everyone has something they're hiding. And there is usually a good reason for doing so. But occasionally, you can find someone to confide in and that's all you need to realize what you have to do. Whatever it is, I won't breathe a word to anyone."

Kate shifted, studying Avery through narrowed eyes. "Really?"

She could hear the skepticism in her own voice loud and clear. Giving in to that part of her that longed to have someone who she could talk to was a bad idea—a *very* bad idea. But what could Avery do, really? They were all leaving tomorrow, anyway.

Heaving a sigh, she rested her head against the barn and closed her eyes. "Houston and I aren't really married."

She'd expected a gasp or some indication that she'd surprised Avery. But there was no reaction. A peek out of the corner of her eye confirmed Avery was still there, she hadn't left. Nor did she seem shocked, dismayed, or disappointed.

Kate continued. "We weren't even dating when we got here. The reason we came doesn't matter—what matters is that while we were here, our feelings for each other shifted."

The corners of Avery's lips lifted. "That tends to happen here, doesn't it?"

The warmth returned to Kate's cheeks. If it was any lighter in the barn, she wouldn't have been surprised if Avery made a comment that her face resembled a ripe tomato.

"Yeah. I suppose it does." She adjusted to sit cross-legged and let her hands rest in her lap. "That's not even the thing I'm worried about. People can make long distance relationships work, I've seen it over and over. But both people have to be supportive and *want* to do the work."

"True."

"That rodeo star, Tyson Lee, saw me rope that calf and he said I have a natural talent."

Avery snorted. "I don't know how you did that. But I'd tend to agree." She pressed her lips into a firm line. "Am I correct in assuming the reason you're in here all alone and in the dark has something to do with your talent for roping calves not meshing with your newfound romantic interest?"

Kate tapped her nose. "Tyson said he's putting together a team and if I was interested, I'd be welcome."

"And Houston isn't thrilled." Avery sighed. "That's tough."

"Yup."

Avery tilted her head and gave Kate a steady stare. "What does your heart say?"

A bark of laughter escaped Kate's throat. "My heart says I'm in a win-lose situation no matter what I choose to do."

"How do you figure?"

Kate let out a dry chuckle. "Because if I choose to stay with Houston, I'll always wonder what might have happened if I had taken that leap and done something unexpected. If I choose to go, then I lose the relationship I just found."

Avery's brows creased. "You're probably right."

"About what?"

She blew out a long, slow breath through pursed lips. "When you said I wouldn't be able to give you advice on your situation."

Kate stared at her dumfounded, then the two of them laughed. "Well, that's just great."

Avery nudged Kate with her shoulder. "You want to know what I did?"

"What you did? Does that mean you went through something similar?"

"In a sense." Avery smiled. "I had to make a choice between my career and the man I was falling in love with."

"Obviously, you picked love." Kate's wide-eyed stared prompted another laugh from Avery.

"Actually, I made the wrong choice. I was so caught up in what I wanted that I didn't see what was right in front of me." Avery leaned in a little closer. "Now, that isn't to say *my* right choice is the right one for you. Everyone is different. You're young yet. You have a whole life ahead of you and a world to explore if that's what you want to do. And if Houston wants to be with you after all is said and done, then he's the right guy for you."

"And if he doesn't?"

Avery lifted a shoulder. "Then he isn't. I'm a firm believer that what is meant to be will happen. Sometimes, you might be the one making the wrong decision. Sometimes, it will be the one you have fallen in love with. But either way, one of you will keep the two of you heading down the right path."

Her dream-like smile warmed Kate from her stomach all the way to her fingers and toes.

"Lucky for me, Logan knew exactly what we needed, and I came around after realizing what I'd lose. You just have to decide to follow what will make you happy."

Kate worried her lower lip. "I was afraid you'd say that." Her stomach knotted. "My whole life has been spent on a ranch. This is the first time I've ever gone more than twenty minutes from home. I have been so utterly sheltered. I know I need to broaden my horizons before I can be the woman Houston deserves. I just don't think he sees that."

"Sounds like you've already made your choice."

Nodding, Kate swallowed hard. "I think I have."

Avery patted her knee. "I wish you every bit of happiness, Kate. I'm going to say one last thing on the matter."

Chest tightening, Kate stilled. Here was the judgment. She should have picked love. Now she'd look foolish if she changed her mind and stayed with Houston.

"It is never too late to take a different path. Do what makes you feel whole. And if you discover you aren't as happy as you hoped to be, listen to what your heart is telling you." She got to her feet. "For what it's worth? I think the two of you make a very handsome couple. I wouldn't be surprised in the least if Houston told you he'd wait for you."

There was a cold, hollow feeling inside her now. If she had to confront Houston about this decision she'd made, Kate knew she wouldn't follow through. She had to charge forward with her plan or she'd chicken out. It would be best to leave a note and ask for forgiveness later.

She had to do this—to be the best possible version of herself. Not for Houston, but for Kate.

CHAPTER TWENTY-TWO

HOUSTON PACED IN THE HOTEL'S CONFERENCE ROOM, HIS arms folded. A feeling deep inside his gut urged him to go find Kate. What if she needed him? Worse, what if she decided to leave without saying goodbye?

He shook off that fear. There was no feasible way she could leave tonight. At the earliest, people would be leaving in the morning. Who would want to start a trip this late in the day, anyway?

Jake sat at the conference table on the opposite side, his hands typing away at his computer then dragging his mouse around. His focus remained on the screen, though Houston couldn't figure out *how* based on his own frenzied emotions. At the rate he was storming through the room, it was very possible that he'd burn a hole in the commercial grade carpet beneath his feet.

"How long is this going to take?"

Jake's eyes bounced to meet his before dipping back to the computer. "I'm searching through our footage to find the specific ones I was talking about. We've recorded several hours. It might take a little longer than I originally thought."

Houston bit back a retort. Part of him didn't think he needed to see this footage. But the more he thought about it, the more he realized that Jake had a point. Kate definitely didn't appear to have the same level of anxiety she'd had when they'd arrived.

The triggering event had been when she'd wrangled that calf.

In that moment, she'd shined, and it was like the protective shell she had around her had been cracked. She'd been able to puncture it, and through adversity, she'd grown stronger.

That thought both terrified him and thrilled him. He'd loved her when she was shy and needed to use him as a shield. And the more she came into herself, the more beautiful she'd become. Still, it was hard to accept, especially when he wanted to be that person she'd depend on. He thrived on being needed.

What if she went on this rodeo tour and came home to realize she didn't need him anymore?

His stomach churned and nausea mixed with the poison being created by his nerves. He didn't want to risk that. It was one thing to grow together and build each other up. It was something else entirely to watch her evolve while he remained stuck in the same rut.

Was that why he had been so insistent on changing his ranch? It was like everyone around him was getting what they'd always wanted and yet his own desires remained just out of reach. He was coming to a conclusion about something, but it was foggy and hard to visualize.

"Ah. Here we go." Jake patted the chair beside him. "Now, we've got about two hours of proof here—more if you pay attention to her in the background."

"Two hours? I don't have time—"

"Easy, tiger. You don't have to watch all of it. I'll just show you the highlights. But do yourself a favor and watch this like you don't know her. It'll be hard, but I think you'll get the most benefit out of it." Jake punched the button on his mouse and leaned back in his chair, lacing his hands behind his neck. "I've put them in a reel. When you've seen enough, all you have to do is push the skip button."

The clips started with their arrival. Kate had practically clung to his side the whole time. Even when he'd wandered off to speak to other people, it was like her focus never left him. Her eyes followed him like she was worried he'd disappear from her sight. "She looks sick to her stomach," he murmured.

"I know. This was definitely a challenge for her."

Kate hadn't wanted to come, not really. If he focused on their conversations leading up to coming to Silverstone, Houston could recall several instances when she'd shown her fear over leaving their home. "I shouldn't have pushed her."

"I respectfully disagree." Jake pushed a button and the clip jumped to another one. He pointed to the screen at Kate during the dance. "This was after you two left. She came back, and already you can see her demeanor shifted quite a bit. Whatever happened after you'd left with her gave her a boost of confidence."

The kiss.

Houston bit back a smile. That kiss had been something else, and completely not what he'd expected.

Jake fast-forwarded through some more scenes and stopped the video. He brought his focus to Houston. "This is when she ropes that calf. Watch her face—the determination, the excitement, every fine nuance."

He pushed play and Houston did exactly what he'd been told. Kate practically glowed. It was almost ethereal.

"The rest of the footage shows only small adjustments. We could tell she was coming into her own, and honestly, we don't think it was *just* you."

Houston's brows puckered as he swung his attention around to peer at Jake head-on. "What?"

He leaned back in his office chair and gestured toward the computer. "Kate is in her natural element when she's working with horses. People make her nervous, but not you—not in the same way, at least."

Houston glanced back at the computer. "Why are you telling me all of this?"

Jake swung his chair lazily from side to side. "It's like I said. At Silverstone, people discover things about themselves than they ever knew. Sometimes it's love. Sometimes it's something more."

Dragging a hand down his face, Houston fought the urge to demand the guy talk less cryptically. Whatever vague reason he had for asking Houston to come look at these videos needed to be more specific. "Can you just tell me why you want to show me these clips? I get it, this place can change someone's life if they want it to."

Jake steepled his fingers beneath his chin. "You're seriously not getting it. *Look* at her." He spun the computer around and pointed to an image of Kate triumphantly sitting beside a roped calf. "Is that the face of a woman who battles anxiety on a daily basis?"

Houston's eyes swept over the screen. Jake had paused it at just the right moment to show off Kate's bright eyes and wide smile. Her cheeks were flushed slightly but she looked radiant. That memory was so clear and the emotions that returned just by looking at the picture were enough to rip his heart out and quash any thought of making Kate listen to him.

"Ah. There it is."

Houston's gaze swiveled back to meet Jake's.

"You see what I'm talking about, don't you? That, right there, is proof this place changes people. For Kate, it allowed her to discover who she was behind the mask she wore." He leaned forward and scrolled through the clips. The screen flickered fast, images blurring, making it difficult to see who was being recorded. Then, Jake managed to stop it at just the right place. One more click, and Kate's smiling face filled the computer.

Jake's voice came in from somewhere off-screen. "When did you realize you loved Houston?"

Kate glanced down at her lap and a smile tugged at her lips before she lifted her face once more. "When he let me wrangle that calf." She paled. "Wait, I didn't mean that—"

Jake clicked the mouse again, freezing the screen just as Kate's features went from stark white to red.

Houston couldn't tear his attention from the computer, as much as he wanted to give Jake a dirty look and have him push play again. "She loves me," he murmured.

"Of course she does. I'm sure she's told you."

"Well, yeah. But how often do we say, 'I love you, too,' just because someone else says it first?"

"True." Jake rubbed his jaw but didn't seem to have much more to say.

Houston blindly reached for a chair and pulled it out from under the table before settling into it. He squeezed his eyes shut and pinched the bridge of his nose. His head pounded along with his heart, and everything ached from his head to his toes. "What should I do?"

Jake chuckled. "Why are you asking me that?"

Houston scowled at him. "I thought the whole point of you bringing me up here to look at your computer clips was for you to teach me something."

Another low laugh, which was really starting to grate on his nerves. "Houston, I brought you up here to prove my point. Silverstone can teach you a lot about who you are and what you want in life. The question is, what have you learned?"

Houston put his head in his hands as he rested his elbows on the table with a thump. "I have to let her join the rodeo," he muttered. When he brought his focus back to Jake, the guy had one brow lifted.

"Do you really think you can do that?"

Lifting his shoulders in defeat, Houston sighed. "What choice do I have? I can't very well say that I love her only to stand in the way of her happiness, can I?"

Every part of his soul ached with this realization. Kate had never been happier than when he'd seen her win that competition. Even when they spent time together, she didn't seem to have that glow he'd seen in that clip.

It was what she wanted, and all he really wanted was to make her happy—even if that risked his own happiness. Houston got to his feet and held out his hand.

"It was a pleasure meeting you, Jake. I wish you luck on your article." He turned and headed for the door, but Jake's voice stopped him.

"I do have one more question for you, Houston."

Without turning around, he murmured, "What's that?"

"Why did you come all the way out here? Why lie about your relationship status? I understand if you had wanted a free vacation for you and someone special. But the two of you weren't in a relationship. You were just co-workers."

Houston grimaced. Deep down, he wondered if there were clues to the feelings he'd developed for Kate so quickly. It didn't make sense that he'd fallen for her so fast. But Jake was right. He hadn't come to take Kate on a romantic getaway.

He cleared his throat. "I wanted to prove you wrong."

"Pardon?"

Then he turned so he could answer Jake to his face. "I wanted to come here with someone I never thought I would fall in love with so I could prove that this place wasn't magic. People don't just fall in love when they come here. Otherwise, there would be a spike in divorces when the 'love' wore off."

"And what did you find?" The wry smile on Jake's face was almost enough to make Houston walk out of there and ignore the question altogether.

"It's like what you and Ben have said. This place isn't magic in the sense that you find love. But it's still special. Whether it's the activities, or the ambiance—or the people." A small smile touched his lips. "Either way, this place seems to be instrumental in helping people figure out what they need in their life most. For Kate, that would be the rodeo. I'm guessing it will be the place that makes her feel most at home."

Jake's features pinched momentarily. "Where does that leave you?"

Houston shrugged. "The rodeo isn't forever. Maybe after she's done living her dream, we can live mine."

He left the hotel, hands deep in his pockets. His heart felt like it was bleeding even though he knew he was making the right decision.

Kate needed this, as much as it hurt for him to put his wants on hold.

There was still music and visiting in the garden when he strolled past the entrance. Kate was probably already at the cabin, and he would have to figure out a way to tell her he was wrong and she should go for it, without sounding like an idiot. Maybe they could come up with a plan for something long distance since she'd be doing a lot of traveling.

The air felt colder somehow as he arrived at the carriage and boarded for the ride back to the ranch side of the property. He glanced back at the impressive lit-up hotel. This place was pretty special. It wasn't like anything he'd expected. It was hard to try to comprehend a way to make Hickory Hollow anything like it.

That was an impossibility, and he was a fool for letting it take him so long to realize it. Silverstone wasn't amazing because of the hotel or the ranch. It wasn't special because famous people ran it. Yes, this place had made a name for itself because of its owners, but that wasn't the reason Silverstone *worked*.

What *really* made this place amazing were the individuals who were here on a daily basis—both the regulars and the visitors. That was the only thing he could think of to make sense of any of it. It was the relationships, both romantic and friendly, that helped people to grow and progress toward their greatest potential.

When Houston made it to his cottage, he waited on the doorstep for a few moments. He could do this. No matter how hard it was, he'd tell Kate that he wanted her to be happy and to follow her dreams, whatever they might be.

Her happiness was more important than anything else he could think of.

He took a deep breath and entered the living room. The whole building was dark except for one lamp that sat on an end table near the love seat. It was quiet—too quiet. His heart leapt into his throat and he shook off the feeling that something was wrong.

The small white piece of paper beneath the lamp's glow caught his attention and he made his way over to it. Without picking it up, he read Kate's neat handwriting.

I WANTED to wait for you to tell you goodbye, but I knew if I did that, you'd convince me I shouldn't go. I love you, Houston. More than I ever realized was possible. But I have to do this. I can't really explain it, but it's like a part of me always knew this was the path I would take. I hope you can forgive me. –Kate

HE SHOULD BE SHOCKED. He should feel anger or additional pain from her betrayal. But all he felt was numb. This was what he'd wanted for her, wasn't it? He wanted her to do what made her happy.

Houston couldn't help but notice she didn't mention anything about keeping in touch or trying to maintain the relationship they'd started. She'd broken up with him though a letter. But he wouldn't let it end that way. No, already he was planning a way to reconcile everything and support her from home.

Long-distance relationships weren't ideal, but he'd figure out a way. He had to.

CHAPTER TWENTY-THREE

KATE HAD NEVER FELT SO SICK TO HER STOMACH. BUT WHY? She was making the right choice. At least, she thought she had until she got into the truck with some of Tyson's other crew members.

Last night, she'd scribbled out a note for Houston, gathered her belongings, and slipped over to the main house.

She still couldn't believe that the people living there had willingly let her into their home. Yes, she slept on the couch—well, that wasn't true. She'd tossed and turned on the couch, but not due to the discomfort. She couldn't stop thinking about the way she left Houston. She was a coward, and he would never forgive her for it.

Trees passed by her window in a blur. The people in the truck chatted excitedly about their first stop. The man sitting beside Kate assured her that there would be plenty of time for her to practice before entering the competitions. They wouldn't expect her to sign up for the first one.

For some reason, that statement rubbed her the wrong way. She was more than capable of holding her own. They didn't need to give her special treatment. But instead of speaking her mind, she simply nodded and offered them a smile she prayed looked more gracious than biting.

If Houston had been here, he would have stood up for her. He would have told each and every one of these guys that she was talented and capable, and they shouldn't underestimate her.

Kate heaved a sigh and turned her attention out the window. She hadn't called Dakota yet—something she'd planned on doing once she couldn't turn back. The farther and farther she got from home, the tighter her chest became and she had to keep repeating in her head that this was the right choice. How was she ever going to grow and become someone she was proud of if she couldn't strike out on her own?

By the time the sun started to dip on the horizon, Kate still hadn't gotten up the nerve to call Dakota or Houston. She'd gotten several text messages from Georgia, though. Apparently, Houston had filled them in. Most of Georgia's messages had been asking if Houston was lying. But then they shifted to something more congratulatory, if not wistful.

The truck pulled into the ranch where the rodeo was to be hosted and everyone piled out. Kate held her phone in her hands and stared at the lit screen. She couldn't wait until tomorrow. Dakota deserved to know what was going on.

Taking a deep breath, she tapped the call icon and found Dakota's number, then lifted the phone to her ear. It rang only twice before Dakota answered.

"Kate? I was wondering when we'd hear from you." There was tension on the other end. Or maybe it was purely imagined. "Houston said something about you taking up with Tyson Lee."

"He's—" Her voice cracked. "He's right. Tyson invited me to come along with his group to a few rodeos over the next few months."

"That's… great, sweetheart." Dakota genuinely sounded supportive, but there was something lingering beneath that tone—something she wasn't conveying. She cleared her throat. "I sure hope you don't run off and become too famous to visit."

Kate sucked in a sharp breath. "Of course not. I—" Holding back the emotion in her voice was proving difficult. "That's the reason I called. I wanted to apologize for leaving so abruptly. I wanted to ask if you'd be okay with me coming back… when this is all over."

Her voice grew quiet. "You will always have a home here, Kate. Don't you ever think otherwise."

Tears brimmed behind Kate's eyes and she brushed at them preemptively. "Really?"

"You're family, Kate. No matter where you go or for how long, we will always be here when you're ready to come home." She seemed to hesitate and the sounds in the background on her side died away, like she was wandering away from them. "I do want to ask you one question."

"Yeah?" Kate's heart thundered, picking up tempo so quickly she almost thought she might have to lie down.

"Does this have anything to do with Houston? The two of you left together and everything seemed fine, but then he came back and he's—"

"No!" She shut her eyes and gave a sharp shake of her head. "Everything is fine between Houston and me. I just realized a few things about myself—I can't keep living under a rock."

There was a long pause on the other end.

Had Houston said something?

Kate wrapped one arm around her waist and grimaced. "This tour should only last a few weeks. Then I'll probably get it out of my system and I'll be coming home."

"Just let us know if you need anything."

Forcing a smile and hoping it translated into her voice, Kate nodded. "I will." A tear slid down her cheek. "Dakota?"

"Yeah?"

"Thank you. For *everything*."

"Of course, dear."

It sounded so silly even in her head, but she couldn't keep the words contained. "I'll make you proud."

"You already have."

The background noise returned, but Dakota didn't speak again. Kate pulled the phone away from her ear to stare at it, as if that would clear up her confusion. When she brought her phone back to her ear, her whole body went hot and cold all at once.

"Kate?" Houston's voice sounded so far away. There was a twinge of sadness in it that made her feel even worse about the whole situation.

"Hi, Houston."

The background noise faded again as he presumably wandered away from his family. "I was wondering if you were going to call—hoping you might."

She shut her eyes tight. "I should have never—"

"I understand."

"I—wait, what?"

He let out a heavy sigh. "I get it. You left because you had to. It was like there was something pulling you toward this adventure. Who am I to stand in the way of that?"

Chills swept through her like wildfire, tingling and pricking in an almost pleasant way. "You really think so?"

"I really do." His voice lowered, doing nothing to stop the chills. "I can't say I was pleased with how you left… but honestly, I think even that was for the best."

This wasn't anything like she'd thought he'd react. The way she'd left had been the absolute worst. "Why?" Kate blurted the question before she could analyze it. A small part of her really wanted him to admit that he wanted her to stay so badly that he would have stood in her way. At this moment in time, she almost wished he had.

Houston chuckled. "Because I saw first-hand the way every light inside you illuminated when you wrestled that calf to the ground. You've never been so completely in your element before. It was truly breathtaking, Kate. I would never want to stand in the way of that for you. And…" He let out a strangled kind of sound. "I don't know if I would have been able to watch you go without making a complete and utter fool of myself."

His voice dropped to a whisper. "I still love you, Kate. I'm so in love with you that it took everything in my power not to call you a dozen times since I found your note and beg you to come back to me."

Her hand slapped over her mouth, fighting the urge to let out a tearful confession that she would have been completely okay with him doing so. "I love you, too. Joining Tyson's rodeo team was never supposed to be permanent. It was just a way for me to grow a little more— to be the woman you deserve."

Boy, that sounded dumb—*so* dumb. She shut her eyes as the blush crept through her face.

He let out another warm chuckle. "Don't you get it, Kate? You might have realized that there was something missing in your life when we went to Silverstone, but I realized something different."

"What did you realize?" She barely spoke over a whisper. He probably hadn't even heard her. Or maybe he had because he didn't miss a beat.

"I realized I had everything I ever wanted and more. It was right in front of my face, and I was too blind to see it."

She sat there, soaking in the words he was saying. Was he referring to her? Or was it something else? Kate didn't dare ask him to clarify. It would simply be mortifying to find out that he'd meant something about the ranch. Heck, she was in some random truck at a ranch she'd never visited before when she probably should have been with him.

"I mean you, Kate."

She swallowed hard. The pounding of her heart intensified. "What?" she murmured.

"You. I fell so hard and fast, and it doesn't matter if this tour takes a few days, months, or even years—I will be here waiting for you when you come home. And if you don't, I will do what it takes to track you down. We share something I can't explain. It's just—"

"I know what you mean." She pressed her lips together, another tear trailing down her cheek, but this time it was a happy one. "Do you really think you can wait for me?"

"I have no doubt whatsoever." He sighed. "I just wish we could have figured this out sooner. Then maybe I wouldn't have to practice my patience."

"What patience?" She snickered.

His quiet laugh joined hers. "Touché."

If their sense of humor wasn't enough to convince her they were made for each other, then the companionable silence they shared on a phone call while being hours apart should have been.

"I love you, Houston."

"I love you, too," he offered. "When you come back, you'd better be prepared to be wooed. I'm going to woo you so hard and fast your head will spin."

Her whole body warmed, like he was right beside her giving her the best hug she'd ever experienced. "I don't have any doubt of that."

CHAPTER TWENTY-FOUR

OVER THE NEXT FOUR WEEKS, HOUSTON BARELY GOT ANY sleep. He was up before the sun and went to bed long after. He had no idea just how long this current rodeo tour would last and he wanted to make sure he had everything perfect, right down to the yellow stars.

He'd brought up the idea of putting together a garden to his mother the afternoon he'd come home from Silverstone. He'd fully planned on giving her a seven-part explanation as to why it would be beneficial to the ranch, despite their lack of tourism.

Surprisingly, she hadn't batted an eye. He had a sinking suspicion she'd seen right through him when he'd arrived home. Maybe it was a mother's intuition. He'd wandered inside and with two words, she'd managed to break the careful wall he'd erected around himself.

"Where's Kate?"

He'd managed to get out a curt explanation regarding the rodeo before stealing away to his room and pulling out his computer.

Building the trellises for the vine walls he wanted to put in had been the most time-consuming part of the whole thing. And they wouldn't be filled in for a few more seasons yet. But he'd managed to get his hands on several wildflowers as well as plenty of native Texas plants.

Houston placed his hands on his hips and surveyed the progress he'd made so far—with the help of some of the ranch hands, of course.

The gardens were not nearly as beautiful as the ones at Silverstone, but he knew in his heart that Kate would love it. The garden wasn't the only surprise he was working on. Yesterday, he'd officially gotten the approval from his parents to start looking into adding onto their ranch, but not in the way he'd originally planned.

Nope, those original ideas would never have been executed successfully. What he wanted to do was far more different than a dude ranch. He wanted Hickory Hollow to add on classes for tykes to learn how to become real rodeo cowboys. And who better to teach them than a woman who was great with kids, albeit a little shy around adults, who also had an affinity for rodeo activities and had even competed in a few of her own?

All he needed was the green light from the woman he loved.

A low whistle sounded behind him and footsteps padded over. Georgia stood at his side and surveyed the small getaway. "You've never worked this hard to impress a girl before. What's up?"

Houston snorted. "I'm in love and you know it."

She bit back a smile and glanced at him out of the corner of her eye. "Apparently." She headed past him down a stone path toward a modest fountain—one he'd bought secondhand.

"Well?" he demanded.

"Well, what?" She set her innocent gaze on him—a look he never fell for.

"*Well*, do you think she'll like it?"

Georgia smiled. "Of course she'll like it. This is totally her thing." She wandered toward a section of yellow stars. "You seem to really like this flower. Why are there so many of them?"

"Because they're her favorite."

Georgia lifted one eyebrow. "Geez. I knew you had it bad, but man, you take this to a whole new level."

His brows furrowed as he took in all he'd been able to accomplish over the last few weeks. "Is it too much? I knew it was too much. I shouldn't have bought the fountain, she's going to think that—"

His twin tossed back her head and let out a laugh. "Have you ever heard of a woman complaining when the guy who loves her goes all out? I don't think so. I guess I just haven't wrapped my head around how serious the two of you have become. It's hard to picture true love when I've never seen it firsthand." She made a face. "Then again, maybe I don't want to see that."

Houston stifled the urge to dig his elbow into her side. Already he was second-guessing everything. He didn't need Georgia to pile on. He took in a deep breath as if it would help quell the nerves inside him. He had to get this right. It might not be the official first impression she'd have of him, but it was the first one she'd have after they'd been together—well, apart, but together all the same.

"Did you hear what's going on at Bolton Ranch?"

He gave her a side-eyed glance, her question a little out of place. The only times she brought up the Boltons were when she had something judgmental to say about their cousins. He moved to inspect one of the yellow stars, not really interested in what she had to say but knowing she wouldn't drop it.

"Does it have something to do with one of our cousins?"

"More than one." Georgia's lips twitched like she was holding back a delicious bit of gossip. "Grace came home."

His brows lifted. Grace had practically disappeared a few years ago. He'd always thought being the oldest and the one to inherit the ranch had been too much pressure for her. Maybe he was wrong.

"And that's not all. Apparently, she's *involved* with someone. I only know part of what's going on, because all Mom can talk about is Ashlyn."

"What does Ashlyn have to do with Grace finally coming to her senses?"

"She's *engaged*. Can you believe it?" Georgia laughed. "It figures that the baby of the family is going to be the one to mess up her life like that."

Houston brows pulled together. "Maybe she's in love."

His sister huffed. "There's no way she can know that. She's barely into her twenties. I guarantee she's up to something. Or she's a little brainless and they'll be divorced in under a year. Too many people get involved in relationships before thinking it through." Georgia met his eyes. "You're different. You and Kate have known each other forever. And you're more mature."

It was like she was trying to backtrack her statement.

"And you went through all this trouble *and* a long-distance relationship. If you can get through that, then you can get through anything." She put her weight on one foot and placed her hand on her hip, blowing a strand of hair out of her eyes. "Do you know when she's going to be back?"

He couldn't say he wasn't disappointed with the shift in topics. Houston shrugged. "They didn't have a specific time. All I know is that they will be coming this way some-time next week." He shot a look in Georgia's direction. "Why?"

Her features scrunched up and she tilted her head. "Didn't Uncle Chad say they were hosting a last-minute rodeo over at Bolton Farms this weekend?"

Houston waved her off. "Yeah? So?"

Georgia moved closer to him and poked him in the stom-ach. He grunted as he jumped back. "Do you think Kate might be at that one?"

"I doubt it. She would have told me."

Or would she? Knowing her, she probably didn't want to jinx any opportunity to be an up-and-coming rodeo star. His presence might throw her off her game, especially since they hadn't seen each other in person for weeks.

"I know that look. You don't *know* if she's going to be there and you're worried that she didn't tell you because she didn't want you there."

He tried to brush off the fact that she was one hundred percent correct. Georgia had hit the nail on the head. If Kate didn't want him at the shows where he could actually attend in person, did she even really want him in her life at all?

Houston cleared his throat. "I'm not going to assume that Kate had any plans one way or another. They might have sprung this one on them last minute like they did for Uncle Chad."

Georgia studied him, her eyes assessing every little tick that occurred in his face. "It's okay to be nervous, Houston. It shows how much you care about her. I think it's actually kinda sweet and I'm pulling for you both."

He swallowed hard. "Thanks," he murmured.

Her gaze swept back over their small garden oasis. "This place is perfect." Georgia's eyes landed on him once more and she offered him an encouraging smile. "I'm going to head in for dinner. You coming?"

Houston shook his head. "I think I'm going to plant a few more flowers before I lose daylight."

She nodded and turned around to head out of the garden. He'd made sure to put the garden close enough to the buildings to be easily accessible, but far enough away that he could add onto it as much as he wanted to in the future. Kate would see it the second she got back to Hickory Hollow.

A silly grin crossed his features. She *would* love this place. Even if their relationship was doomed to fail, she would always have an escape.

He stooped to pick up a tray of buttercups and moved farther into the gardens. It wasn't an elaborate maze like the one at Silverstone, but that didn't matter. It hadn't been designed to impress thousands. This place was made with only one person in mind.

Houston stopped beside a bench he'd hauled out to the gardens, positioned beneath a mature oak tree that hadn't been torn down to make way for farming. It was the perfect place to sit in the shade during the hotter months.

He knelt down and stabbed his trowel into the soft earth. A few more flowers and he'd call it a day. And maybe he'd look into the rodeo that his uncle was hosting. If it turned out that Kate would be there, maybe he'd surprise her— after her competition, of course.

A quiet gasp ripped through the air, and he whirled around to find a pair of familiar brown eyes staring in awe at the gardens that surrounded them. Kate's hand covered her mouth, preventing her from letting out any other sound.

He remained frozen. She looked different. Her chestnut hair had grown out a little and the waves framed her face.

Her skin was more bronze, as if she'd spent more time than usual out in the sun. When her bright eyes shifted down to him, something about them made his breath hitch in his chest. There was a confidence he hadn't seen before —like she was prepared to take on the world or more.

Kate was the most breathtaking creature he'd ever seen.

Houston dropped the trowel in his hand, and it clattered against the stone he knelt on. In one fluid motion, he rose. "Kate. You're—back."

She tucked a strand of hair behind her ear and gave him a shy smile. "Sorta."

His brows creased. What was that supposed to mean? Was she going out on another tour? His stomach lurched at the thought. This was only supposed to last for a couple weeks. Tyson couldn't expect her to continue traveling when she had a home and a family that missed her.

He shoved those selfish thoughts aside. Kate was the only one who could make those decisions, and Houston had already decided he wouldn't make her choose between him and the love she'd developed for the sport.

Kate shifted her weight from one foot to the other, her hands shoved in her back pockets. She nodded to their surroundings. "So, what's this?"

A sound that resembled a snort and a cough escaped his throat. "What does it look like?"

She seemed to be fighting a smile. The corners of her lips twitched as she looked around the gardens. "It looks like you've been busy."

He took a step toward her. "Yeah."

"I guess it really stuck with you that I had a soft spot for flowers."

"Obviously," he murmured, still moving closer.

"And it looks like you wanted to give me a reason to stay."

There was that hint to the fact that she might be leaving somewhere again. His chest tightened and he slowed his steps. "Do you need a reason? Because I can give you several."

The smile broke across her face and she tilted her head slightly. "Maybe." Her tone was teasing, and it made his heart skip a beat. His heart was being yanked in one direction and then another—like it couldn't decide whether to be excited or terrified over the path this conversation had taken.

As much as he wanted to move closer to her again, he kept his feet planted firmly where they were. Sure, he could pull her into his arms and beg her to stay here, to continue to grow and develop by his side as their relationship continued to progress. But he wasn't about to do any of that without knowing if she was on board.

Kate moved toward him and stopped with just a foot between them. He could smell her perfume, which caused a fresh ache to overwhelm him. Her lashes fluttered and she looked down for only a moment before she brought her gaze up to meet his.

"Why did you put this garden together, Houston?" she whispered.

He shook his head; she didn't have to ask. It was clear he'd done it for her. He let a chuckle rumble through his chest before he grasped her chin with his finger and thumb.

"Because I love you and I wanted you to know how much." He motioned to their surroundings. "But to be honest, this place doesn't come close to expressing what's in my heart."

Her eyes brimmed with emotion. "It says more than you realize, Houston." A tear slipped down her cheek. "I have been to several ranches over the past month, but at each one I can safely say I could never get rid of that feeling of homesickness."

She reached up and placed a hand against his cheek. "But it's not the ranch, the horses, or even the beautiful gardens or surrounding properties. There was always something missing and now that I am here with you, I can say honestly that it was you—you're my home. You're the one that makes me feel like I belong." She let out a teary laugh. "And, of course, your family. I've been able to see a lot of what the world has to offer even in the short time I've been gone. I've met all kinds of people, too. But Hickory Hollow will always be my home and where I belong."

Houston was suddenly very aware of the thundering beats his heart was making. "You're staying?" he rasped.

"Of course, I'm staying." She laughed again. "But there's one more show I have to attend. And there's something I need to talk to you about."

His brows creased. "Okay?"

She dropped her hand from his face and stepped a little closer. It was almost like he'd already developed a habit of putting his arms around her. He slipped his hands around her waist and pulled her even closer.

Kate grinned at him. "The last rodeo on our tour is at Bolton Farms."

Figures.

She continued. "I want you to come with me."

"Of course. I'd do anything for you, Kate."

"Really? Because there's something else…"

Houston pressed a kiss to her forehead then pulled back and met her eyes again. "I said anything, and I meant it."

Kate pressed her lips together tightly. "I've been thinking about it a lot. From the first time you kissed me to how everything has developed over the last month. I don't want you to think that I'm being ridiculous or—"

"Kate," he laughed, "just spit it out."

"Will you marry me?"

His mouth dropped open and his eyes rounded. He could have sworn his heart stopped because every part of his body went weak.

That wasn't how this was supposed to go. He was supposed to be the one to propose to her. In fact, he'd planned on doing it in this very garden when he knew she was ready. He'd even picked out a ring.

Her features pinched and she looked away. "I'm sorry. It was too soon. I shouldn't have—"

Houston hooked his finger under her chin and lifted it. *"Anything,"* he repeated before he dipped to seal his promise with a kiss.

EPILOGUE

K<small>ATE</small> <small>STOOD</small> <small>ON</small> <small>A</small> <small>BALCONY,</small> <small>LEANING</small> <small>AGAINST</small> <small>THE</small> wrought-iron banister thirty floors above the Silverstone gardens. She could see the yellow stars from this vantage point, and the sight brought a smile to her face.

Her gaze shifted toward where the ranch was located through the trees. If she focused really hard, she could see horses being led by the cowboys to and from the barn. Houston had insisted they spend most of their time over at the ranch because it was the place where he'd realized his love for her ran deep.

She couldn't agree more. Silverstone was more than just a dude ranch where people came to find love. It had been the trigger to help her thrive. It had helped her find a confidence she never knew she had. And it had brought her Houston.

His arms came around her, his hands resting on the banister, framing her in. Houston's nose nuzzled her neck, sparking an electrical current and the accompanying chills that ran up and down her spine. His warm breath tickled the hairs on her neck. "Good morning, Mrs. Shipley."

Kate smiled, leaning into him and closing her eyes. "Good morning, Mr. Shipley," she murmured.

He turned her around to face him, keeping her locked within his arms. "What do you want to do today?"

Kate lifted her gaze to meet his. "I was thinking we might sneak off to the barn today—reenact a certain first kiss I'm fond of."

His lips quirked into a smile. "I'm game for that."

Then she frowned and glanced over her shoulder. "Wait, I forgot I promised Tyson that I'd help him take a look at a few of his recruits."

Houston wrinkled his nose. "But it's our honeymoon. Can I convince you to do it later?" He leaned in closer, his intention to kiss her fully apparent.

She shook her head and pushed two fingers against his chest. "If you want me to retire, I have to help him fill my spot. Besides, you know how good I am at picking out natural talent."

"You're pretty amazing," he concurred. "Those kids you teach back home are lucky to have you." He brushed a kiss along her jawline and hummed his pleasure. "But not as lucky as I am."

Kate smiled. "You're just lucky that the magic here hasn't died off. Didn't I say this place was special?"

He rolled his eyes but smiled at her all the same. "I still think it's ridiculous."

"Houston!" She laughed.

He pressed a firm kiss to her lips, then pulled back with a heart-stopping grin. "Maybe it's not magic. Maybe it's destiny."

GET YOUR FREE COWBOY ROMANCE

If you love sweet cowboy romance, you'll love this freebie too. Join my readers group and you'll receive a copy of *Finding Her Cowboy* as my gift to you.

This stand alone story is an enemies to lovers whirlwind romance set in small town Texas where Thatcher Ranch and Bolton Ranch meet.

The Brothers of Thatcher Ranch series and the Billionaire Ranchers series comes together with cameo appearances by characters in each one.

Get a taste of each sweet romance series when city girl Adelaide and cowboy Maddox fall in love in the rancher's world Addy shouldn't fit into, but does.

https://dl.bookfunnel.com/nyfq5715yh

APRIL MURDOCK BOOKS

Silverstone Dude Ranch

Cowboy's Redemption

Cowboy's Surprise

Cowboy's Competition

Cowboy's Fate

Cowboy's Challenge

Cowboy's Assumption

Cowboy's Myth

Cowboy's Rival

Cowboy's Destiny

Billionaire Ranchers Series

Impressing Her Billionaire Cowboy Boss

Keeping Her Billionaire Cowboy CEO

Saving Her Billionaire Cowboy Hero

Loving Her Billionaire Cowboy Partner

Arguing With Her Billionaire Cowboy

Teaching Her Billionaire Cowboy Rookie

The Brothers of Thatcher Ranch

The Cowboy's One and Only

The Cowboy's City Girl

The Cowboy's Troublemaker

The Cowboy's Second Chance

Wealth and Kinship

The Billionaire's Heart

The Billionaire's Hope

The Billionaire's Generosity

The Billionaire's Loyalty

The Billionaire's Sincerity

The Billionaire's Promise

Silverstone Ranch

The Movie Star Becomes a Cowboy

The Cowboy gets a Second Chance

The Chef Chases His Cowboy Dream

The Billionaire Tries the Cowboy Life

The Royal Cowboy Chooses Love

Texas Redemption

A Long Road Home for the Broken Ranger

Sweet Second Chances for the Reluctant Billionaire

New Inspiration for the Lonely Rockstar

A Change of Plans for the Youngest Son

A Rude Awakening for the Ambitious Ex-Boyfriend

Small Town Billionaires

The Billionaire's High School Reunion

The Aimless Billionaire

The Billionaire's Charity Date

The Beach Bum Billionaire

The Grouchy Billionaire

The Billionaire's Home Town

Christmas Miracles

Her Undercover Billionaire Boss

The Billionaire's Family Christmas

Christmas Carols for the Billionaire